EMPRESS WU ZETIAN

First edition. September 26, 2024.

ISBN: 979-8227788122

Written by Nangong Bo.

Empress Wu Zetian

III

Written by Nangong Bo

Translated by Cheng Shuiying

G reat Wall Publishing

Chapter 15

Seven ministers, including Dee Renchieh, the Prime Minister and Minister of the Central Secretariat; Pei Hsingben and Ren Chihgu, two Ministers of the Central Secretariat; Pei Hsüanli, the Minister of Finance; Lu Hsien, the left Assistant Minister; Wei Yuanchung, the central Assistant Minister; and Li Szuchen, the Governor of Luzhou, were all suddenly arrested and imprisoned by the subordinates of Lai Chü nchen on the same day. The news of the seven ministers being arrested on the same day spread, causing panic in Luoyang, as people were unaware of what major incident had occurred.

The Southern Yard has increased the number of guards from the Golden Armored Guard.

The Northern Gate, informed by Lai Chünchen, has assigned a Guard General to take charge of the daily duty.

The situation has put the Great Zhou Palace on high alert as if facing a major enemy.

The Empress resided in the Five-Phoenix Pavilion within the Western Garden, seemingly oblivious to the tense situation beyond its walls.

Four or five ministers who requested an audience to present their petitions were all advised to avoid it. This was a rare occurrence after the Empress ascended the throne, and every minister in the court knew that although the Empress's private life was dissolute, she was always decisive in political matters. What was the reason for today's unusual situation?

They were waiting outside the palace gates.

And then Wu Chengsi (Prince Wei) entered the Palace.

The ministers watched as the Empress's nephew entered the Palace arrogantly, and they all had uneasy thoughts.

The Empress on the top floor of Five-Phoenix Pavilion, wearing a loose-fitting robe, sat on a cushion lost in thought, while Wan'er recited documents beside her - a very leisurely scene.

Wu Chengsi went upstairs, and the relaxed atmosphere was immediately disrupted.

The Empress looked at her nephew, her expression turning serious and profound.

"Is that true? Did you investigate?"

"Your Majesty, I have investigated!" Wu Chengsi bowed with a look of sincere anxiety and fear, "The evidence has not been found yet, but there are reasons behind this. Dee Renchieh and Wei Yuanchung both claim to be former ministers of the Tang Dynasty, intending to restore their old sovereign."

"Do they have any actions of rebellion?"

"Your Majesty, they are plotting a rebellion." Wu Chengsi said with certainty.

"Oh."

"Your Majesty, we were fortunate to have uncovered the conspiracy before it happened. Otherwise, their actions would have been even more powerful than those of Hsü Chingye." Wu Chengsi continued seriously, "There are actually seven ministers in the court who are plotting treason at the same time. "

"Oh!" she sighed again.

"Your Majesty, the truth will be revealed through interrogation."

"I know," she said regretfully, "I know..."

"Your Majesty, the interrogation is ready."

She nodded, then sighed.

"Dee Renchieh and his gang were all people I cultivated personally. I raised them from obscurity to prominence, entrusted them with important tasks, but unexpectedly they conspired against me when they gained some power."

"Your Majesty," Wu Chengsi said with a gloomy expression, "people's hearts are

truly fickle!"

"Well," she sighed, "you can go and tell whoever wants to see me for the sake of the seven ministers that there's no need to do so. Just wait for the outcome of the trial.

I also have to wait for the outcome of the interrogation before making a decision."

"Your Majesty, I'll notify Lai Chünchen to interrogate them."

"Tell Lai Chünchen, do not be unjust or lenient!" The Empress's tone was very harsh, as if a peach pit was stuck in her throat.

"Yes!" Wu Chengsi bowed and took a step back.

"You inform them, do not mistreat the seven ministers." the Empress said, lowering her head, as if filled with infinite sorrow.

After seeing Wu Chengsi walk out, Wan'er continued to recite. However, the Empress was no longer in the mood to listen. She raised her hand to stop Wan'er and then said sorrowfully:

"I never expected that even Dee Renchieh would turn against me."

"Your Majesty, the matter has not been revealed yet." Wan'er replied casually.

"It can't be fake - if Lai Chünchen is not sure, he will not act recklessly! Over the years, almost all cases related to rebellion have been true. People are always unhappy to see a woman as Emperor, no matter how well I treat them, like Dee Renchieh..."

Wan'er knew that the Empress had ambiguous feelings towards Dee Renchieh. Therefore, when the Empress mentioned him repeatedly, she dared not speak up. The Empress was truly saddened by Dee Renchieh's rebellion against her. After a moment of silence, she sighed softly and ordered Wan'er to summon the Zhang brothers.

Encountering depression in reality and facing problems without immediate answers, she tried to escape in order to relieve her stress.

She sought to numb herself with pleasure and forget about reality. In the past, she used to confront reality head-on, always exploring further when faced trouble. But now, she seeks temporary escape to avoid the trouble and disturbance.

Wan'er had served the Empress for a long time and understood her temperament. At this moment, she suddenly felt that the Empress had taken another step closer to old age - avoiding, because her energy was not enough to cope with heavy issues.

After the Zhang brothers entered the Palace, Wan'er retreated to the outer chamber. She had heard too much about rebellions, and now she was almost numb. Since the Empress came to power, there had been rebellions almost every year. And each case was proven to be true. Because of the past experience, Wan'er had developed a concept in her mind that she thought all rebellions were doomed to fail, but people still rebelled, which was a fact.

She had a quite good impression of Dee Renchieh. However, this positive impression was influenced by the Empress rather than intuition. Therefore, she neither had intuitive sympathy for DeeRenchieh's rebellion, nor did she have as much emotion as the Empress.

Shortly afterwards, Lai Chünchen suddenly appeared and met Wan'er in the outer chamber, inquiring about the Empress's intentions regarding this case.

"Wu Chengsi has informed you, and the Empress has no other instructions,"

Wan'er replied casually. "Do you have anything else to report?"

"This is the matter. The Empress is resting; I will come back later." Lai Chünchen made a bow, turned around and exited. But before he crossed the threshold, he turned back and asked, "Do you know what impression the Empress has of Yang Zhirou, an Assisting Minister of the Central Secretariat?"

Wan'er was clever and immediately sensed the hidden meaning in the words. Naturally, she was unwilling to involve herself in the power struggle. So, she just smiled faintly and shook her head, saying:

"I have never heard the Empress mention him."

"That's it," Lai Chünchen smiled satisfactorily and then bowed to Wan'er, "I will

go interrogate immediately. If the Empress inquires, please speak on my behalf."

Lai Chünchen was a notorious demon in the court. Any case, once it fell into his hands, would be quickly concluded and the expected confession obtained. He had all kinds of cruel punishments, and he could also intimidate the environment with his power. The people of Luoyang were terrified of him. Now, Dee Renchieh and his six companions were led to the hall. When they saw the devil sitting high up, they realized that their fate was sealed and there was no turning back. So Dee Renchieh signaled to Ren Chihgu with a glance, indicating that there was no need for futile protests.

Lai Chünchen sat in a dignified manner, watching as seven prisoners were brought in one by one. He smiled grimly and turned to the judge Wang Deshou on his left, saying:

"You go prove their identities!"

So Wang Deshou got up from his seat, accompanied by four scribes, holding the ledger in hand, called out the names of each person, and then returned to the front to report to Lai Chünchen:

"The seven rebels, Dee Renchieh, the Prime Minister and Minister of the Central Secretariat; Pei Hsingben and Ren Chihgu, two Minister of the Central Secretariat; Pei Hsüanli, the Minister of Finance; Lu Hsien, the Left Assistant Minister; Wei Yuanchung, the Central Assistant Minister; and Li Szuchen, the Governor of Lu'chou, were verified without error."

After Wang Deshou returned to his seat, Lai Chünchen waved a hand to issue the first order: prepare the torture instruments.

So, more than thirty warriors brought out the torture instruments from the two corridors and displayed them in the hall as a demonstration, also shouting and yelling.

This was a vulgar demonstration. Dee Renchieh looked at Lai Chünchen who was sitting arrogantly in the seat of honor and couldn't help but sigh.

At this moment, Lai Chünchen issued a second order, commanding his attendants to strip the seven guilty ministers of their robes and hats.

Dee Renchieh remained calm and did not protest against the order to remove his official robes. However, Wei Yuanchung, the Central Assistant Minister, protested loudly, saying, "Lai Chünchen, according to the rules of the dynasty, ministers should

not remove their robes before the verdict is rendered."

Lai Chünchen glanced at him disdainfully and said coldly:

"I have never rendered an unjust verdict in my judicial career!" He paused for a moment and added jokingly, "If you are innocent, I shall kneel before you seven and dress your robes."

Next, the gavels of the left and right judges were struck, followed by the muted ringing of the wooden bell outside the court.

And then Lai Chünchen rose slowly from his seat in the middle.

"I was appointed to investigate this major case of treason by imperial order - Her Majesty had issued an edict, stipulating that those found guilty upon first interrogation would have their sentences reduced." He paused, his voice rising, "Consider your actions first. If you confess yourselves, I shall beseech Her Majesty for mercy and a lesser punishment."

With his speech concluded, the bailiffs on either side raised their instruments, issuing a loud cry. Following that, they struck the ground with their wooden clubs, producing a resounding thud.

Dee Renchieh was filled with infinite sorrow and anger. In his mind, the Empress was wise. However, the fact that the Empress appointed Lai Chünchen, such an unworthy person, was digging her own grave. Dee Renchieh considered himself loyal to the Empress, but he also understood that it was pointless to argue in front of an arrogant villain. He also realized that he and the other six people were all old, and even if they did not die, they would be disabled if they were tortured. Therefore, he decided to bet on fate, hoping to escape ordeal today in the hope of rectifying their wrongs in the future.

This was an inevitable decision. And thus, with a profound voice, he said solemnly to Lai Chünchen who was sitting in the upper seat:

"Please give me paper and brush..."

"Once you confess, there will be someone recording it," Lai Chünchen continued sternly, "This is my usual way of handling cases, and it cannot be altered for the sake of Lord Dee." After he finished speaking, he chuckled and gestured to the scribes on his left and right, "Get ready!"

Dee Renchieh coolly gazed upon Ren Chihgu and Pei Hsingben, whispering:

"What transpired today cannot but be acknowledged, in anticipation of some hope ahead!" As he spoke, his eyes swept over the torture instruments on both sides.

Ren Chihguo and Pei Hsingben also understood the situation and nodded in agreement.

Thereupon, Dee Renchieh took two steps forward, stood straight, and gazed directly into Lai Chünchen's eyes with his bright and piercing gaze. In that fleeting moment, he did not resemble a captive, but rather a deity descending to earth, majestic and serene, unafraid of the impending fate.

The sturdy countenance struck fear into the heart of Lai Chünchen, who dared not meet Dee Renchieh's gaze. He averted his gaze.

Thus, Dee Renchieh began his discourse in a clear and resounding voice.

"The Great Zhou Revolution brings about a renewal of all things, the former ministers of the Tang dynasty willingly accept punishment, acknowledging the truth of rebellion."

These simple sentences were clear and melodious with a tone of dominance. Lai Chünchen, despite his prowess in manipulating situations, finally found himself at a loss for words. He forced a smile and said:

"Good, good, you have confessed it yourself, well done! I will definitely plead with the Emperor to spare you from the death penalty," he said, then turned to Ren Chihgu, "What about you?"

"The Great Zhou Revolution brings about a renewal of all things, the former ministers of the Tang dynasty willingly accept punishment, acknowledging the truth of rebellion." Ren Chihgu repeated it once more.

Lai Chünchen smiled, waving his hand as he said:

"With these two tough ministers admitting it, the major part of the case has been settled, and the preliminary trial is over..." he said, bowing to Dee Renchieh, "Your Excellency is very cooperative. "

Dee Renchieh stood resolutely, unmoved.

"Well then, bring back the seven elders for further interrogation. "

"I have something to say." Wei Yuanchung, the Central Assistant Minister, suddenly exclaimed with indignation.

"You..." Lai Chünchen shrugged. "You can speak next time, the major case was settled for today."

"I did not rebel, I was framed by villains," Wei Yuanchung exclaimed wildly, "I did not betray, I know, neither did the other six."

"Wei Yuanchung!" Lai Chünchen's face changed. "Do you wish to die sooner?" "I have long put life and death out of mind."

"Old crook!" Lai Chünchen slammed the table, "Doesn't know what's good for you!"

At this moment, Hou Sichih walked in and said to Lai Chünchen:

"Let me take care of this fearless crook for you!" After saying that, he sat down on the right side of Lai Chünchen and shouted, "Guards, hang Wei Yuanchung upside down first!"

"Yuanzhong!" Dee Renchieh called out in a low voice, "Today..."

Wei Yuanchung signaled Dee Renchieh with his eyes to stop and turned to Hou Sichih with a sneer, asking, "Are you planning to hang me upside down?"

"Yes, that taste is really good!" Hou Sichih chuckled.

"Is that so?" Wei Yuanchung also smiled, "It's no big deal. I have always had a tough life and have experienced setbacks before! Once, I was riding a donkey on the road, and accidentally fell off the saddle. My foot got stuck in the stirrup, and the stupid donkey dragged me along for quite a distance."

"Damn it," Hou Sichih cursed angrily, "You scoundrel, how dare you act so recklessly in front of me, I'll immediately use the leg vise to snap your legs."

"You may use the leg vise, but this will not intimidate me! Hou Sichih, even if you bring a sword to cut me apart, I shall not flinch. But if you think I will admit to treason voluntarily, forget it, because fundamentally there is no such thing."

"Bring forth the leg vise!" Hou Sichih let out another roar.

"Bring forth the leg vise!" Wei Yuanchung imitated his tone and called out.

Hou Sichih was in a state of confusion, but Lai Chünchen remained calm. He observed Wei Yuanchung and knew that the latter was determined to die. What Lai Chünchen wanted was a confession, even a simple one admitting to the facts of the rebellion. Details could be clarified later. Therefore, he raised his hand to stop Hou Sichih from using the leg vise and said:

"Details can be further investigated. Let's stop here for today," he said, waving his hand repeatedly, ordering the guards to take the ministers away.

Dee Renchieh and his companions filed out one by one, all looking serious. In front of the escorting judge Wang Deshou, they did not speak.

Upon returning to the prison cell, Pei Hsingben found that Wang Deshou was talking to the jailer, so he whispered:

"Falling into the hands of Lai Chünchen, we will surely not end well. We must

find a way to report to the Empress."

"Yes, today I admitted to the rebellion, but it's just to buy some time. We need to come up with another plan. Only by appealing to the Emperor can we be saved." Dee

Renchieh said in a low voice.

"How can we report to the Empress while in prison?" Pei Hsingben asked, looking despondent.

Dee Renchieh glanced at the jailer and the judge, suddenly took out a handkerchief from his sleeve, and at the same time, bit his little finger, using blood to write a character "injustice" on the handkerchief. He quickly pulled open the seam of his robe, carefully stuffed the blood-written handkerchief into the cotton, then slowly flattened it, closed the seam, and tied a knot.

Pei Hsingben didn't understand why, and watched in confusion.

At this moment, Judge Wang Deshou came over, Dee Renchieh slightly moved his body and murmured softly:

"The weather has warmed up, and the prison cell is not ventilated. Judge Wang, please send a guard to take my cotton-padded jacket back home, instructing my family to remove the cotton and replace it with a padded shirt to be sent in."

Wang Deshou looked at him and nodded slowly.

"Certainly - you're too thrifty, changing the cotton-padded jacket for a padded shirt is just common among small households, rarely seen in your noble family."

"I was born in a poor family, so I got used to it. It's not that I intentionally live frugally," Dee Renchieh calmly took off his cotton jacket and handed it to Wang Deshou, then bowed and said, "Thank you, Judge."

Wang Deshou did not suspect anything unusual about the cotton-padded jacket, so he took it and handed it to his attendant to take away.

Soon the prison cell fell silent. Pei Hsingben slowly moved closer to Dee Renchieh and whispered softly:

"I hope this cotton-padded jacket can work miracles."

"I am just doing my best, whether my family will report our issue while seeing this one word, it's hard to say for now."

At this moment, Ren Chihgu slowly approached and inquired about the situation, saying in a deep voice:

"Our fate is not very optimistic. It is those princes of the Wu clan who instigated Lai Chünchen to frame us. The Wu clan will definitely sow discord in front of the Empress. With the Wu clan inside and Lai Chünchen outside, it will not be easy for us

to survive."

"As long as the Empress can personally interrogate, we still have a chance," Dee Renchieh firmly believed in Wu Zhao, and he continued confidently, "The Empress will not be as reckless as her nephews."

The prison cell was dim, and a night passed.

The next morning, Judge Wang Deshou personally brought the padded shirt for Dee Renchieh and pulled him to a corner, whispering, "Lord Dee, the Empress's favor towards you is extraordinary. Chünchen really wants to exonerate you. If you are willing to implicate another Assistant Minister Yang Zhirou, then, Your Excellency may be spared from death."

Dee Renchieh listened quietly without saying anything.

"Lord Dee, this is a once-in-a-lifetime opportunity." urged Wang Deshou.

"Judge Wang!" Dee Renchieh stood up straight and shouted loudly, "Heaven and Earth can witness my loyalty. I am not afraid of death, but why do you want me to falsely accuse innocent people!"

"Lord Dee!" Wang Deshou was intimidated by his momentum and dared not approach again, saying cautiously, "I'm just saying it for your sake, nothing else."

"If it's for my sake, I'd rather die in front of the Empress." Dee Renchieh said, and then he threw himself against the wall of the prison.

Wang Deshou rushed forward in a panic, grabbed Dee Renchieh, and quickly said: "Lord Dee, please don't do this. I will take my leave now and wait quietly for the imperial decision." he said, cupping his hands before walking away in embarrassment.

Dee Renchieh looked at his companions with a melancholy expression and said in a deep voice:

"They want to get rid of all the honest officials in the court in one fell swoop."

"Lord Dee, as planned, your jacket has returned, and your son must have received that blood letter. He should go to court this morning to report the situation."

"Perhaps..." Dee Renchieh's confidence wavered as Wang Deshou appeared, suspecting that the princes of the Wu clan and Lai Chünchen had already set up a trap,

and that his son might not be able to enter the court to report the situation.

Yes, Lai Chünchen had the power to do so. As long as he took precautions in advance, Dee Renchieh's son would have no way to report the misconduct of the case. However, Lai Chünchen's was too confident. He thought that since Dee Renchieh had confessed personally, with numerous crimes piled up, there was no possibility of exoneration, so he did not make any arrangements to take a step back.

Dee Guangyuan, the eldest son of Dee Renchieh, took advantage of this gap to achieve his goal of reporting the misconduct.

Wu Zhao saw in sorrow a word "injustice" written in blood on a handkerchief. She was puzzled and summoned Dee Guangyuan, asking gently:

"Where did you get this blood letter from?"

"My father sent this handkerchief from prison. It was hidden in the cotton. After I obtained it, I hesitated for a long time before daring to report it."

Dee Guangyuan said in pain, "I beg Your Majesty to judge clearly, my father will never rebel."

Wu Zhao looked at Dee Renchieh's blood letter, pondered repeatedly, unable to find an answer. She had already learned that Dee Renchieh had confessed to rebellion in person, and now, she saw his blood letter. Which aspect was the truth between the two?

"I will fairly adjudicate this case."

Although Dee Guangyuan, who had reported the incident, had left, the Empress's thoughts were still fluctuating. She summoned Lai Chünchen to inquire:

"Chünchen, how did you interrogate Dee Renchieh and his group?"

"Your Majesty, none of them have been tortured, and they have been treated as well as possible. Their clothing and headwear have not been removed..."

Wu Zhao gestured to stop Chünchen from speaking, then asked again,

"How did they confess?"

"It was Dee Renchieh who confessed first, admitting to the rebellion. Among the seven people, only Wei Yuanchung, the Central Assistant Minister did not admit guilt. Hou Sichih wanted to use torture instrument to force a confession, but I stopped it. I believe that harsh methods should not be used in interrogating high-ranking officials.

Fairness must be sought, or else it will breed slander."

Wu Zhao agreed with the opinion of Lai Chünchen and solemnly instructed:

"You should find the judge for further interrogation, and must not act hastily."

After making this arrangement, the Empress's mood improved slightly, but the fundamental regret still existed. She speculated about Dee Renchieh's thoughts based on her own, thinking that the confession was the truth, while the blood letter was a personal request. She thought, "Dee Renchieh wouldn't be unaware that I favor him, right?"

After returning to the inner palace, she kept taking out Dee Renchieh's handkerchief to have a look, studying the handwriting, and concluded that the word "injustice" was written by Dee Renchieh in a hurry.

The Empress was troubled and finally she ordered Zhang Changzong to play the flute and instructed the music band to select dancers to perform the Zhezhi dance[1].

- This is to pass the time, to conceal the anxiety in the heart.

However, in the end, her intentions were uncertain.

One day later, she issued an edict dispatching an Attendant of Central Secretariat

to the prison to inspect the situation of the seven ministers.

The imperial edict was written by Wan'er, who discerned the Empress's thoughts and gently suggested:

"Why don't Your Majesty personally interrogate Dee Renchieh and the others?"

She shook her head without giving a reason, and soon pulled out Dee Renchieh's

blood-stained handkerchief from her sleeve.

Just then, two new musicians performing the Zhezhi dance entered.

The Empress raised her eyes and saw two children coming in, one of them looking refined and like a child from a decent family. In a distracted manner, she blurted out, "Who are you?"

The child seemed well-prepared and immediately knelt down to answer when questioned:

"I'm the son of Yue Sihui. My father was wrongfully accused and imprisoned.

Thus I was enslaved in the Palace. "

"Oh," she cast another glance at the blood-written letter in her hand, and her imagination took flight. She pondered, "It won't be long before Dee Renchieh's children are also consigned to the Palace as slaves."

The child knelt straight, tears streaming down from his eyes.

Wu Zhao looked at his tears, finally unable to bear it, waved her hand and said:

"I forgive you!"

"Your Majesty, I humbly request to clear my father's name of any wrongdoing."

"Your father?" Wu Zhao exclaimed, "He confessed to plotting rebellion himself."

The child kneeling on the ground with wide eyes, in an instant, seemed to be filled with anger reaching to the heaven, and said passionately:

"Your Majesty, in all cases handled by Lai Chünchen, no one dares not to confess. If Your Majesty doubts it, you can select a loyal and upright minister from the court to be interrogated by Lai Chünchen. Each one will turn out to be a traitor."

The child's indignation took Wu Zhao by surprise, and she asked solemnly:

"How old are you? Who told you about Lai Chünchen like this?"

"I am nine years old!" The child was still furious, answering in a high voice, "Your Majesty, you are wise and perceptive. Do I need someone to tell me about the actions of Lai Chünchen? Your Majesty, the court officials, and the people of Luoyang all knowthat Lai Chünchen uses harsh laws to frame the innocent."

"Youngsters shall not speak ill of the ministers!" The Empress spoke solemnly in order to maintain the dignity of the court.

"Your Majesty, with your wise and benevolent rule, even though I may face death, I must speak the truth today. My father has passed away and our family is in ruins, but I must take the opportunity to present my case."

The child's stubbornness finally softened the Empress's heart, and she began to doubt about the approach of Lai Chünchen handling the case. She then ordered the chamberlain to take the child away, and turned to Wan'er, saying:

"Summon Dee Renchieh and his group to me, I will personally interrogate them."

Just then, Choulin, the Attendant of Central Secretariat as special envoy in charge of investigating prisons, entered to report back.

"Let him in!" the Empress said to the chamberlain, her voice trembling slightly. She had no reason to fear, but at this moment she felt a sense of disappointment. Dee Renchieh, whom she favored, was accused of rebellion, while Lai Chünchen, whom she trusted, was portrayed so unfavorably by a nine-year-old child. Neither of them may be true, but they all left her confused and troubled.

Choulin, the Attendant of Central Secretariat, entered the Empress's living room in the inner Palace.

"How is it?" The Empress was slightly nervous.

"Your Majesty, Dee Renchieh and others have a memorial of apology for death to submit." Zhou said, handing over the memorial with both hands.

A chamberlain took the memorial and placed it in front of the Empress. These
words made the Empress's heart sink. She glanced at it and asked:

"Have they all pleaded guilty?"

"Yes," Choulin nodded firmly, "The memorial of apology has made everything

clear."

She lowered her head as if reading the memorial on the tablet, but in fact, she couldn't see anything, regretting - in her heart, she hoped that Dee Renchieh's rebellion was just a misunderstanding, with no evidence to support it.

At the same time, she hoped that Lai Chünchen was not as bad as the child described, imagining that he was just too strict in enforcing the law.

But Dee Renchieh's memorial of apology for death shattered her first fantasy.

After Choulin retreated, the Empress looked at Wan'er and said bleakly:

"There are many things that make me sad."

"In the case of Dee Renchieh and the other ministers, Your Majesty personally presiding over the trial may reveal other issues." Wan'er consoled with an ambiguous tone.

"The memorial of apology has been submiteed, why bother to personally review

it?" She said wearily, "My kindness to others has only brought me misfortune."

"Your Majesty, the chamberlain has taken the imperial decree to summon Dee Renchieh and the others - should we send someone to bring them back?"

In theory, when the memorial of apology has already been submitted, it's unnecessary to personally review it. However, Wu Zhao felt sentimental at this moment. She thought, since they have been summoned, she might as well meet them and see the person she secretly favored. So, she softly said, "No need to retrieve it - I'll question them again."

Shortly afterwards, the seven ministers were summoned into the inner palace and waited in the corridor outside the hall.

It was not appropriate to hear cases in the living room. Wan'er requested the Empress to come to the central hall and sit on the throne to receive the audience.

She hesitated for a moment, and finally said reluctantly:

"I'm too lazy to move, I'll just stay here."

"Your Majesty," Wan'er, knowing the Empress valued ceremony, reminded, "It seems as if we are here neglecting..."

"No problem," said the Empress with a slightly sinister tone, "have them prepare

- and summon Zhang Yichih to keep evidence."

Therefore, Zhang Yichih, the Deputy Minister of the Legislative Bureau, set up a

small table on the left side of the imperial desk. Eight chamberlains held ceremonial axes and stood behind the Empress, while Wan'er sat at the small table on the right side.

In addition, four palace maids on both sides served as recorders.

Wan'er and the others got ready, then struck the gong to announce the summoning.

Outside the living room, there were twenty-four chamberlains standing on both sides in the corridor, reporting one by one after the gong sounded.

And then fourteen chamberlains escorted seven ministers, walking in a line, and stopped outside the door of the imperial living room. The Chief of the Imperial Harem reported to the Empress:

"Criminals Dee Renchieh, Ren Chihgu, Pei Hsingben... are waiting to be summoned."

The door curtain was lifted, and the seven ministers entered in single file, bowing to the Empress.

Wu Zhao was in a state of depression, but when the seven people entered, she suddenly became spirited, gazing at everyone calmly and clearly, and asked,

"You rebelled..."

"Your Majesty, we have been falsely accused and implore Your Majesty to clear our names!" Dee Renchieh seized the final opportunity and spoke out loudly.

The other six people also cried out for injustice one after another.

Wu Zhao's gaze swept across the faces of everyone, lingering on Dee Renchieh for a longer time due to psychological reasons. In that brief moment, she felt that her initial impression of Dee Renchieh remained unchanged - this person would never be

involved in conspiracy or rebellion. Therefore, she solemnly but calmly asked:

"You are here to plead your case, but you have already confessed," she turned to

look at Wan'er and whispered, "Read out their confession."

"The Great Zhou Revolution brings about a renewal of all things, the former ministers of the Tang dynasty willingly accept punishment, acknowledging the truth of rebellion." Wan'er recited calmly.

"Is this your confession?" the Empress asked.

Dee Renchieh responded "Yes" loudly, and then said solemnly:

"This simple confession was uttered by me. At that time, under the interrogation of Lai Chünchen, if one did not confess first, they would be subjected to torture and humiliation until death. In the interrogation by Lai Chünchen, everyone has confessed. Your Majesty, please think carefully-even if we were plotting rebellion, we would never confess immediately without seeking to cover up the truth. We are only doing so out of fear of torture and death. At that time, we hoped for a day like today."

Wu Zhao thought of the words spoken by the son of Yue Sihui...

"Your Majesty," Wei Yuanchung continued, "I swear I am not plotting treason.

However, Hou Sichih ordered to hang me upside down."

"Hmm!" Wu Zhao responded heavily, then asked, "If you confess and accuse each other, it is because you fear torture. So why did you submit a memorial of apology for death? Choulin, the envoy in charge of interrogations, will not use torture instruments on you."

Dee Renchieh turned to Ren Chihgu, Pei Hsingben, and others, and replied in surprise, "We have not yet submitted a memorial to apologize for death."

"Wan'er, show them the memorial."

Two chamberlains held up the memorial and presented it to Dee Renchieh. After

only reading two lines, Dee Renchieh called for Ren Chihgu to look at it together.

"Your Majesty", Minister Ren Chihgu only glanced at it and exclaimed loudly, "This is the handwriting of Judge Wang Deshou. Your Majesty may summon him to testify."

Wu Zhao was taken aback and looked back at Zhang Yichih.

"Take a look at the handwriting."

The memorial was handed to Zhang Yichih, who looked at it and said straightforwardly:

"Your Majesty, this is a handwritten letter from Wang Deshou without any falsehoods."

"Did you not ask Wang Deshou to write it for you?" Wu Zhao's face was very serious.

"Your Majesty, none of us is inferior to Wang Deshou in literary talent. Why do we need Wang Deshou to write for us?" Pei Hsingben said firmly.

"Your Majesty, Wang Deshou once ordered me to make a false charge against Yang Zhirou, a Minister of the Central Secretariat, saying that it could reduce my crime and avoid death," Dee Renchieh continued in a painful tone, "I have served Your Majesty with devotion, and always uphold justice, be loyal to my duties, never form factions or seek flattery. I have been implicated in this rebellion case without knowing the causes or the facts. The situation is confusing, and I hope to clear my name today, regardless of life or death." Dee Renchieh spoke with a tone of sorrow, tears streaming down his face.

"Minister Dee!" Wu Zhao sighed.

"Your Majesty, from Wang Deshou's unauthorized submission of the death memorial on behalf of me and others, you can see everything. We are innocent and were forced by the threats of Lai Chünchen..." Pei Hsingben kowtowed loudly, passionately spoke out.

The Empress glanced at Zhang Yichih, then turned her gaze to Wan'er, and said slowly:

"Read once more the original confidential report."

Wan'er opened the case file and slowly read aloud:

"Lai Chünchen reports - according to the confidential report from the East Garden... further verified by the investigation of the Chief of the Golden Armored Guard in the Southern Yard... Minister Dee Renchieh, Minister Ren Chihgu, and Pei Hsingben... conspired together with solid evidence, attached with the original investigation report at the end..."

The Empress listened attentively and raised her hand to stop Wan'er before she finished reading. Then, she sighed and spoke to the seven people with emotion:

"Over the years,there have been too many people plotting rebellion. Although Lai Chünchen was too strict in enforcing the law, many serious cases were solved because of his strictness. You probably still remember the incident that someone had colluded with Hsü Chingye. My reign is newly established, and its foundation is not yet solid. I would rather punish wrongly than let anyone go. If I do, my country and people will completely collapse. Therefore, no matter who it is, if anyone shows a tendency to treason, I will punish him severely."

She paused and continued, "I am willing to live in peace with you, but I hope you will respect my royal authority."

"Your Majesty, we serve with loyalty and without any ulterior motives." Ren Chihgu said.

"Now, each of you can go home," the Empress said slowly, then turned to Zhang Yichih, "Close the case and release them. Let the Imperial Harem send escorts to accompany the seven ministers home. In addition, the son of Yue Sihui will be sent out, and his family members who are enslaved will be pardoned and have their property returned."

Since Lai Chünchen took charge of handling the rebellion case, this was the first time the case had been closed and the people released. When the Imperial Harem escorted the seven ministers back to their residences, it caused a sensation in Luoyang, and officials rushed to spread the news, thinking it was unusual.

The Prince of Wei, Wu Chengsi, was the mastermind behind this case. After receiving the report of the release of the seven ministers, he hurriedly went to the Palace - he wanted to reverse the decision of the Empress. He had his own ideas: "If you don't hit the dog, you will be bitten by the dog." These seven ministers had considerable potential in the court. If they could not be brought down this time, they might turn against him in the future, which would be hard to defend against. Therefore, as soon as

he heard the news, he went to the Palace without hesitation.

After interrogating these seven people, Wu Zhao unexpectedly felt exhausted. She lay on the couch and asked Zhang Yichih to give her a massage.

The manner of Lai Chünchen made her regretful. Now, she rethought what Lai Chünchen had done, thinking that she had been deceived by him.

When Wu Chengsi entered the court, she did not order Zhang Yichih to avoid him. At this time, she tended to take advantage of her age and no longer avoided many things. Sometimes, she would deliberately let people see her with her male attendants, and now, she was in that mood.

Wu Chengsi tactfully expressed his opinion on the seven ministers' rebellion.

"They already have the intention to rebel, although they have not taken any action yet. It's not that they don't want to take action, but rather because of the strict security measures that prevent them from doing so," he paused for a moment before continuing, "Your Majesty's decision to release them, while benevolent, may lead to future trouble as they have not abandoned their ambitions."

The Empress responded with a casual tone, as if nothing had happened:

"The matter has passed, what I said cannot be withdrawn, so there is no need to dwell on it any longer."

"Your Majesty," Wu Chengsi said anxiously, "once this trend starts, I'm afraid that officials like Lai Chünchen may not be willing to give their full efforts in the future."

"I have my own intentions." The exhausted Empress was reluctant to delve deeper into the issue, almost forcibly stopping Wu Chengsi's words.

Later, she sighed and said to Zhang Yichih:

"I am tired."

"Your Majesty, have a good sleep, and you will feel better tomorrow."

Tomorrow, the problem would still exist. The Empress thought about how to deal with Lai Chünchen in the court. Lai Chünchen was a lackey, but she had built up the power of this lackey over a long period of time. Wu Zhao was the one who understood the use of real power the most. So in order to prevent trouble, she took a compromise measure that had nothing to do with reason. When they discussed the case in the morning court, she ordered the Minister of Central Secretariat to announce the disposal of the seven ministers:

Dee Renchieh was demoted to Pengze magistrate, Ren Chihgu was appointed as Jianghsia magistrate, Pei Hsüanli as Yiling magistrate, Wei Yuanchung as Fuling magistrate, and Lu Hsien as Hsihsiang magistrate.

In addition, Pei Hsingben and Li Sichen were exiled to Lingnan for slandering court affairs in their correspondence.

Chapter 16

Upon Wu Chengsi's removal from power, Lou Shide and Li Zhaode were appointed as prime ministers by the Empress, who had bestowed special favors upon them. These two have never been submissive to the Wu clan.

This marked a significant development after the case of the Seven Grand Ministers, as the Empress transferred power from her nephews to outsiders. In the Wu clan, this measure sparked widespread fear, and Wu Chengsi and Wu Sansi personally presented their arguments to the Empress, but the Empress remained resolute in her decision. To her nephews, she said:

"You are both dukes, with ample opportunities for handling various issues. Why dominate the executive position? Moreover, should any issues arise, you can always come to the Palace to consult with me at any time." She paused, then continued: "I intend to broaden my circle somewhat. Relying solely on a few of you is insufficient for governing the nation and maintaining peace in the world."

Empress Wu's measures were unaccountable, and members of her clan dared not defy her decision. Hence, after Wu Chengsi left the court, a new breeze swept through the imperial court of the Great Zhou Dynasty – a bunch of scholars from humble backgrounds, having entered office via Lou Shide's recommendation, were soon dispatched by the Empress to various districts outside the capital.

This measure brought about the grouping of the surviving Guanlong nobility and Shandong clans with the princes of the Wu Clan, as the rise of officials with humble birth posed a threat to them all.

However, the Empress was intrigued by this new measure. As the old aristocratic faction and the Wu clan endlessly harped on its pros and cons, she and the Zhang brothers plotted how to further delve into new talents as the pillars of the new dynasty. In this respect, the Zhang brothers were in agreement with the Empress, as they too hailed from humble origins.

This was an evolutionary trend in the empire. In the past, although Wu Zhao also moved in this direction, her policies were not as clear or active as they were now.

Wan'er, the imperial scribe, recorded the new policies in her daily record book. The Empress summoned numerous newcomers almost every day; some were given posts, while others met with her only once before being dismissed. Those appointed to offices also faced dismissal after serving for three or four months – a newly recruited official had to undergo two entirely different assessments. One was the test of loyalty by Lai Chünchen, the other was the examination of intelligence under the supervision of Li Zhaode. Should either of these two examinations fall short, an instant loss of office would ensue. Over the past half a year, local officials and middle and lower-level officials of the Zhou Dynasty have been changing like a revolving door.

And the newly appointed Assistant Prime Minister Li Zhaode, due to the Empress' personnel management system, had established his own power base. He was gradually able to challenge Lai Chünchen in dignity.

The Empress would summon Lai Chünchen and Li Zhaode every day.

One day, during an audience in the Ming Hall, Li Zhaode suddenly asked:

"If an Assistant Imperial Censor violates the regulations with evidence, which pertains to criminal law, how should the Prime Minister handle it?"

Since the reign of Emperor Taizong, Wu Zhao has been proficient in criminal law and familiar with the statutes. When asked by Li Zhaode, she answered without hesitation:

"According to the laws of our dynasty (following the laws of the former Sui Dynasty), they will be meted out death by caning in the court. If a lighter sentence is given, they will be exiled."

Li Zhaode bowed to the Empress again, without explaining why he was asking.

However, before the early morning court session the next day, Li Zhaode, in his capacity as the Prime Minister, conveyed the imperial order and announced the execution of Hou Sichih the Assistant Imperial Censor by caning.

This was a sudden event, and the officials outside the Zichen Hall were greatly shocked. Normally, the death penalty by caning would not be applied before the morning court session.

When the general of the Golden Armored Guard ordered his subordinate to carry out the imperial decree, Lai Chünchen had to step forward to stop it. Hou Sichih has always been his main assistant and has also gained the trust of the Empress. Lai Chünchen did not believe that the Empress would order the Prime Minister to carry out the execution without going through him first, so he came out to request to wait until the Empress held court before executing the punishment.

Li Zhaode, cunning as he was, bowed deeply to Lai Chünchen, then turned to Lou Shide, another Assistant Prime Minister and Chi Suo, the Captain of Ming Hall, solemnly said:

"I executed Hou Sichih the Assistant Imperial Censor by order of Her Majesty, and Lai Chünchen the Assistant Minister of Grand Court obstructed me from enforcing the law, with you both as witnesses."

Lai Chünchen was taken aback. His power was above that of the Prime Minister, but at the Zichen Hall, his authority could not be compared to that of them. When Li Zhaode spoke in a fierce manner, Lai Chünchen became discouraged. At the same time, he thought of immediately taking the route through the inner palace for help. Therefore, he did not interrupt, turned around, and left.

Li Zhaode knew that Lai Chünchen was entering the Palace to seek support. Without hesitation, he turned around and ordered the golden-armored guards to take action.

When Wu Zhao went to court, the Imperial Censor Hou Sichih had already been executed. Li Zhaode calmly stepped forward, presented the impeachment of Hou Sichih and his violations, including privately storing palace brocade, engaging in witchcraft, hoarding armor at home, and plundering private property. Finally, he spoke out loudly:

"I submitted a request yesterday and received instructions from Your Majesty. I have now followed the orders and enforced the law."

The Empress has received the report from Lai Chünchen. She originally intended to temporarily exile Hou Sichih and then recall him after a period of time. She did not expect Li Zhaode to act so independently, which displeased her. However, she had to admit the reality and reluctantly nodded, saying:

"The execution of the guilty party shall proceed without further discussion. However, Hou Sichih has always been loyal and obedient, so his family members do not need to be further investigated."

Li Zhaode's public assault on the Lai Chünchen clique and the execution of Hou Sichih drew the attention from the entire court.

Wu Zhao made no overt statements about this high-profile case. Theoretically, she could not condemn Li Zhaode; but in reality, his actions left an indelible shadow upon her heart. She harbored a resentment towards Li Zhaode's cunning and dominance. She was a thoughtful politician, but like most politicians, she had a desire to monopolize power. Sometimes she would delegate authority, but more often, she always hoped that power would be wielded by her alone.

She thought that Li Zhaode's execution of Hou Sichih was a cunning attempt to gain power, deviating from loyalty and righteousness, so she was depressed. Whenever she was in a bad mood, she would think of the Mirror Hall - and whenever she was in a good mood, she would also think of going to the Mirror Hall.

However, in the Mirror Hall, she still couldn't forget about the incident with Hou Sichih. In the past, the Empress could hide her emotions deeply, but in the past half year, there have been some changes in her temperament. She would talk about herself incessantly like an ordinary old woman now, and she confided her feelings to Zhang Yichih.

"Your Majesty, why not dismiss him?" Zhang Yichih echoed the Empress's tone, "Someone who seizes power without authorization will bring a lot of trouble in the future!"

"I can't change my Prime Minister all the time," the Empress murmured softly, "Li Zhaode is an upright official who dares to defy Chengsi, and not afraid of Lai Chünchen, which is truly rare."

Zhang Yichih fell silent. When the Empress had conflicting thoughts, he could not offer advice. Moreover, he felt that it was not appropriate to discuss politics in the Mirror Hall.

The Mirror Hall is a place for men and women to enjoy themselves.

So he began to massage the Empress...

She was enjoying herself, watching the illusion created by the mirror, gradually letting herself relax...

In a newly built palace lived the two Zhang brothers: Zhang Yichih and Zhang Changzong. This palace used to be the Ming Hall, and further back was the Qianyuan Hall. Now, the newly built building was called the Tongtian (Heavenly) Palace, which was not as large as the old Ming Hall and the ancient Qianyuan Hall, but the construction was exquisite and surpassed them. Zhang Changzong employed craftsmen as skilled as those who built the Mirror Hall to construct the Heavenly Palace.

The Empress really liked this palace and changed the reign title to "Wansui (Long Live) Tongtian" to match its name.

The owner of the Heavenly Palace was Wu Zhao, but her time in the Heavenly Palace was far less than that of the Zhang brothers.

The Empress ordered them to live in the Heavenly Palace, forbidding them to go out without permission, turning the Palace into a prison.

Now, the two brothers were discussing a newcomer in the Palace - the imperial physician Shen Nanch'iu.

Lately, the Empress has been getting very close to Shen Nanch'iu. The Zhang brothers were discussing whether Shen Nanch'iu would make them fall out of favor.

Zhang Yichih has been serving the aging Empress for a long time and has grown tired. He complained to his younger brother:

"I would be willing to have someone take over for me and let me go out."

"Brother!" Zhang Changzong shook his head and said in a low voice, "You are mistaken. Once we fall out of favor, there is no way we can survive."

"Do you think she will kill us?" Zhang Yichih disagreed with his brother's opinion, "We are different from Hsüeh Huaiyi and we have not stirred up trouble in politics."

"The Empress may not want us to die, but there are many people who hate us. Now, because we have the support of the Empress, others can do nothing about it. Once we leave the Empress's side, everyone will punch us." Zhang Changzong sighed, "In the past, I didn't understand the meaning of being on the back of a tiger and unable to get off. Now, I understand that our current situation is like that."

Zhang Yichih lowered his head. His brother's words made sense. He couldn't help but believe it. Back then, in order to gain fame and fortune, he had used Hsüeh Huaiyi's connections to become the Empress's favorite. Now, trying to break free from this relationship was not easy.

"I have studied Shen Nanch'iu," Zhang Changzong said slowly, "He is different from us, he will not captivate the Empress!"

"How do you know?"

"Shen Nanch'iu relies on medicine - he claims to have various exotic medicines that can rejuvenate people."

Zhang Yichih suddenly burst into laughter...

"This is exactly what the Empress likes. I can tell she is worried about her old age! Alas! How terrible her eyes have become with age! I fear she will soon be unable to see anything."

"In general, the Empress looks twenty years younger than her actual age. It's not easy for an old woman in seventies to look like her. From the outside, she looks like she's fifty, maybe even younger. "

"Hmm..." Zhang Yichih pondered for a moment, and said, "Changzong, I just realized something. The Empress always dresses up when she's with us."

Zhang Changzong was pondering, as if trying to recall if there were any exceptions.

"Whether it's midnight or early morning, she always wears heavy makeup," Zhang Yichih said again, "This is because she doesn't want us to see her old age."

"Perhaps, she relies on cosmetics to conceal her aging," Zhang Changzong shrugged, "Shen Nanch'iu made her look younger for a short period, so he will gain the favor of the Empress, but it won't last long. There is no eternal youth in this world. The Empress is wise, she may be fooled for a short time, but she won't be deceived for long."

"Changzong, we need to find a way to gain our freedom - the current situation is too dire. Being in the Heavenly Palace is no different from being in prison. Besides, once we get outside, someone will follow us. Lai Chünchen is like a pair of pliers, squeezing us tightly. "

Zhang Changzong nodded: "We need to figure out a way, and at the same time, we need to be on guard against Shen Nanch'iu."

Shen Nanch'iu was a new favorite of the Empress, and his encounter with the Empress was very coincidental. Once, Wan'er suddenly had a stomachache, and Shen Nanch'iu, the newly appointed imperial physician, was on duty. He was summoned to treat Wan'er. He did not use any medication, but only massaged Wan'er to relieve the pain. The result was miraculous - after a moment of massage, Wan'er's pain completely disappeared.

This incident left a deep impression on the Empress towards Shen Nanch'iu, and Wan'er also introduced Shen Nanch'iu's lovely craftsmanship to the Empress.

The Empress's interests are diverse, and she thought it wouldn't hurt to have a try. Besides, Shen Nanch'iu was only in his thirties, and although he was not handsome, he was not unpleasant either. As a result, the Empress summoned Shen Nanch'iu to serve her twice.

Shen Nanch'iu used massage techniques from the Western Regions, which were different from those of Zhang Yichih and Hsüeh Huaiyi. Moreover, Shen Nanch'iu took the opportunity during the massage to recommend his own medicine to the Empress.

He told the Empress that applying a certain ointment to the body and then massaging it could prevent skin aging.

Wu Zhao's abdominal muscles have relaxed, and her abdominal skin has developed unsightly wrinkles, so she had a great interest in Shen Nanch'iu's ointment.

Stimulated from the depths of the soul, although Shen Nanch'iu was knowledgeable in many techniques, what he could offer to the Empress was physical, while what the Zhang brothers could offer to the Empress was spiritual.

So, Wu Zhao felt emotional in her joy, thinking to herself, "These two brothers, if they were not my favorites and were placed in the court, would probably also achieve considerable success." This thought arose from her affection.

The presence of Shen Nanch'iu once caused panic among the Zhang brothers, but the aging Empress's love for the Zhang brothers deepened in comparison. She felt that she could not afford to lose them anymore, believing that life would be meaningless without them.

They were professional lovers; they were courtiers. However, due to the affection of the supreme Empress for them, their identities were gradually changing. In the past, Zhang Yichih intermittently read special documents to the Empress, summarized them, and wrote down her instructions, similar to the work of Wan'er. Now, Wu Zhao handed over general matters to the Zhang brothers, which seemed ordinary, but this was power. Wu Zhao, back then, also had such contact with power and gradually grasped it.

Love and joy relaxed the Empress.

When a person comes into contact with power, there will inevitably be a desire to expand.

As a result, there relationship between Zhang Yichihi and Lai Chünchen became subtle.

In front of the Empress, the person who had the most power was Lai Chünchen. Zhang Yichihi could only gain power by taking it from Lai Chünchen. He had already noticed that Lai Chünchen's status in the Empress's mind had declined, so he was scheming that if he could squeeze out Lai Chünchen and obtain some power from him, he would be able to do whatever he wanted in the capital.

Therefore, Zhang Yichihi plotted a conspiracy. He used indirect means to leak information to Lai Chünchen, and then to Wu Sansi - the content being: The Empress was dissatisfied with the Crown Prince and was planning to depose him...

This was not recent news. Since the Empress founded the Great Zhou Dynasty, the issue of the Crown Prince has always existed. Initially, Wu Zhao intended to appoint Wu Chengsi as the Crown Prince. However, due to opposition from the old officials of the Tang Dynasty and the fact that their influence was still significant, she did not dare to act too aggressively and shelved the matter of appointing a member of Wu family as the Crown Prince. In recent years, this issue has not been raised again, but the princes of the Wu clan have continued to spread rumors. There were rumors in Luoyang that the Empress favored Wu Sansi.

With the rumors as the foundation, the information revealed by the Zhang brothers naturally attracted attention, because they were the closest to the Empress, and would always receive some personal information in bed.

Lai Chünchen grasped this information - he knew he was falling out of favor and had to reverse the situation. The only way to do so was to first anticipate the Empress's intentions and then create a major case...

Now, he would take actions against the Crown Prince based on indirect information.

Lai Chünchen has already instigated a group of palace maids to accuse the Crown Princess of using witchcraft.

Following the usual practice, Wu Zhao handed over the investigation of the truth to Lai Chünchen. As a result, the Crown Princess Consort Liu and the Concubine Dou were both executed for their involvement in witchcraft.

Next, the Censorate officials and the Crown Prince's attendants stepped forward to accuse the Crown Prince. Wu Zhao once again handed over the entire case to Lai Chünchen for handling.

But the Crown Prince could not be personally interrogated. After Lai Chünchen was ordered to do so, he brought over a dozen attendants of the Crown Prince for interrogation.

Zhang Yichih was paying close attention to the development of this matter.

When Lai Chünchen was interrogating the Prince's attendants, the Zhang brothers were serving the Empress in the Heavenly Palace.

Zhang Yichih kept staring at the dripping of the bronze pot, and when the time was almost up, he suddenly made a suggestion:

"Your Majesty, Lai Chünchen is going to interrogate the Crown Prince's attendants. Let's go and have a look."

To Wu Zhao, this was not a pleasant matter. She frowned and sighed softly, saying:

"What's so interesting about this?"

"Your Majesty - this is a serious matter, and I think it would be a good idea to learn about the trial in person." Zhang Yichih said implicitly.

Wu Zhao remained silent, sensing that there was a reason behind his words. However, she was still unwilling to listen to the trial herself. Although there was no family affection in the imperial family, Wu Zhao thought it was always unbearable to listen to people confessing her son's affairs, so she sighed slightly and shook her head.

"Your Majesty!" Zhang Changzong pretended not to see the Empress's reaction and interjected, "Let's go quietly and take a look - people say that Lai Chünchen has a terrifying presence when interrogating suspects, making them shiver in fear and confessing to their crimes. Perhaps Your Majesty has never seen this before."

This suggestion caught the attention of Wu Zhao. She was not drawn to Lai Chünchen because of his intimidating abilities, but rather out of curiosity. She wanted to see for herself whether Lai Chünchen's interrogation methods were fair, especially after the case involving Dee Renchieh. She decided to secretly observe and draw her own conclusions.

So the Empress got in a sedan, accompanied by the Zhang brothers, and departed.

Lai Chünchen interrogated the Prince's attendants in a room on the right side of the Su Zhang Hall, which belonged to the inner restricted area. Although in terms of the system, the Su Zhang Gate belonged to the Southern Court and was guarded by the General of the

Golden Armored Guards, the Empress sent internal guards to monitor outside the Su Zhang Gate in order to strengthen the inner restrictions. Therefore, this area could be considered part of the Southern Court as well as the inner restricted area.

The Empress arrived quietly, accompanied by sixteen chamberlains and the deputy Chief of the Harem, and no one was allowed to spread the news. Therefore, Lai Chünchen, who was sitting high at the table, was completely unaware.

More than ten attendants knelt in a circle in front of the table, and an imperial censor read out the indictment and the criminal acts. Then, the censor read out the grace of pardon that could spare one from death based on the confession in the first trial.

At this moment, Wu Zhao arrived and sat with the Zhang brothers behind the screen to watch the trial.

Then the instruments of torture were thrown to the ground, making a terrifying sound. Next, Lai Chünchen spoke:

"You may offer your testimony, but if there is a single false word, I will punish you."

"The Crown Prince has never shown any signs of rebellion".

"Boo!" Lai Chünchen shouted loudly, "These crooks won't speak the truth without torture. Come, clamp each one of them."

The instruments of torture were applied - more than a dozen attendants all let out screams of shock, followed by painful groans.

Just then, one man defied the guards at the threshold and rushed into the courtroom. He held a dagger in his hand and strode menacingly to the front, pointing at Lai Chünchen with a sharp and fierce voice.

"Under the severe punishment, what could not be attained? The Crown Prince has not actually plotted a rebellion, but you have cruelly framed him and tried to put him to death. I am a musician, and I have nothing to do with the affairs of the court, but I can't bear to see the Crown Prince being falsely accused of death, so I would like to cut open my belly here to show my loyalty to the Crown Prince." He spoke as he unbuttoned his shirt and plunged the dagger into his belly.

The event was so sudden that Lai Chünchen had no time to stop it. The musician had already eloquently expressed his thoughts and then decisively disemboweled himself. His action was so bold and fast that everyone present was shocked. Two accompanying imperial censors stood up in a panic and said: "What should we do?"

Lai Chünchen bit his lower lip, hummed, and then said heavily:

"It may be the Crown Prince's assassin causing trouble here. Check if he is dead, then take him away. We cannot let the interrogation be interrupted by a mere musician."

The Empress, who was peeking behind the screen, was moved by the scene and looked back at Zhang Yichih, saying in a low voice: "Pass the word to stop!"

So Zhang Yichih moved the screen aside and went out. At the same time, Zhang Changzong was ordered to summon the deputy Chief of the Harem and the chamberlains from outside the door.

A group of people escorted the Empress into the courtroom.

Lai Chünchen had not expected such a situation. He knelt down in panic to greet the Empress, but the Empress did not look at him and walked straight to the fallen musician. The deputy Chief of the Harem was already examining the musician who had committed suicide, and reported:

"Your Majesty, he is the musician named An Chinzang - his intestines are not injured, there may be a chance to save him."

Wu Zhao saw the wound on his abdomen split open. It seemed that his intestines had spilled out, and she couldn't help but cry out in sorrow and pain:

"I have a son who cannot speak for himself, causing you such distress." She paused for a moment, then said to the deputy Chief of the Harem, "Carry him into the inner palace, and order the imperial physician Shen Nanch'iu to treat him. I want to save his life."

And then the four chamberlains carried away the musician An Chinzang.

The Empress's gaze finally shifted to Lai Chünchen at this moment. She was overwhelmed with sorrow and said somberly:

"Chünchen, you have betrayed my trust."

Lai Chünchen knelt down and kept kowtowing.

Wu Zhao stood still for a while, finally ordered the deputy Chief of the Harem to release the captured attendants of the Crown Prince, and then returned to the Heavenly Palace.

The Zhang brothers succeeded, but they had worried looks on their faces and remained silent. After entering the Heavenly Palace, they both knelt down before the Empress.

"Get up - I know your good intentions," she sighed deeply, "I never thought Lai Chünchen would go so far as to betray me. I haven't trusted my son, but I have trusted a cruel official. Yichih, I appreciate what you have done."

In this way, the situation of the court has completely changed.

The Empress dismissed Lai Chünchen from his position, and then she also dismissed Li Zhaode. Li Zhaode and Lai Chünchen were adversaries, but fundamentally, both were ruthless officials. After Lai Chünchen was removed, Li Zhaode once threatened to exterminate the Lai faction and avenge the wrongly accused court officials. Wu Zhao dismissed him for this reason, and in order to appease the Lai faction and prevent any turmoil, she had Li Zhaode executed.

She used to trust the cruel officials, but after experiencing the trial incident, her views changed. She wanted to change from being tough to being lenient.

So she issued an edict to recall Dee Renchieh.

In her memory, among the ministers in the court, Dee Renchieh was truly a person who could be both lenient and resolute. Therefore, she hoped he would come back. She imagined handing over the political power to Dee Renchieh, using his leniency to remedy the fierceness of Lai Chünchen and Li Zhaode.

Luoyang breathed a sigh of relief at Lai Chünchen' dismissal.

However, Dee Renchieh's return did not attract the attention of the people in Luoyang. After paying his respects, he did not appear in public again.

Dee Renchieh shut himself up at home, refused all social interactions, and stayed alone, planning for his future. He was getting old, with not many days left, but the political situation was too intricate for him to retire. Therefore, he had to plan carefully. The first issue he needed to deal with was Lai Chünchen. As long as this man was alive, neither the court officials nor Dee Renchieh himself could rest easy.

He had been at home for a month when one day the doorman came in to report that Princess Taiping, the most famous princess in Luoyang, had come to visit. Dee Renchieh had no previous contact with Princess Taiping, so he was surprised by this sudden visit and quickly dressed himself to greet her.

Princess Taiping was already waiting in the hall. When Renchieh came out, she greeted him with a charming smile.

"Minister Dee, you wouldn't have expected me to come..."

"I did not know the Princess was coming, please forgive my lack of proper welcome." Dee Renchieh said as he bowed.

"I know you are resting at home," the Princess said with a smile, "I came unexpectedly, can you guess why I am here?" Princess Taiping was solemn when they first met, but immediately turned playful.

Dee Renchieh had an inexplicable feeling as he gazed at the somewhat aged Princess Taiping with a sense of confusion.

The Princess said with a smile, "The Empress wants to see you. Since I am in the Palace serving the Empress, I would like to undertake this errand. Minister Dee, please ride in my carriage to the Palace, okay?"

"I dare not, how can I ride in the Princess's carriage?" Dee Renchieh felt uncomfortable because he was unfamiliar with Princess Taiping. Moreover, the childish appearance of an aging woman disguised as a young girl made him feel uneasy.

"It's no trouble, anyone can ride in my carriage. I asked for permission to come and pick up Minister Dee, shall we go now?" Princess Taiping stood up.

"Okay, then I'll be impolite." Dee Renchieh also stood up, "Princess, since this is your first visit to my humble abode, won't you have a drink?"

"Not today, maybe another day. But I enjoy lively atmospheres. If you want to treat me, you'll have to make it grand. I know you're usually very thrifty." the Princess said kindly and affectionately.

Dee Renchieh was caught in confusion. What happened today was too sudden. He was pretending to appease the Princess while finding out the cause. This mystery was not partially solved until he entered the Palace.

After the Empress received him, she tactfully recounted how she asked Princess Taiping to invite him, and then spoke with an emotional tone:

"My daughter has been spoiled and never considers the consequences of her actions. I hope she can get close to you. She is not young anymore, and I hope she can have a good future."

Dee Renchieh didn't know how to respond. In the long years he had spent with Wu Zhao, this was the first time she had mentioned her daughter. The Empress's family matters involved intricate and complicated issues, and he naturally found it inappropriate to comment.

"I have been very tired in recent years!" The Empress sighed, "You mentioned to me before... that the world is stable now, there is no need for harsh laws. Yes, I also think so. I hope for peace in the future. I am old, although I am not afraid of storms, but calm seas are always the best."

"Yes, Your Majesty!" Dee Renchieh replied in a low voice, "I believe that the days ahead will be peaceful. The chaos of the early days of the Great Zhou Dynasty has become a thing of the past. In history, every dynasty inevitably experiences chaos in its early stages. To give a more recent example, the early years of the founding of the Tang Dynasty by Emperor Gaozu were also chaotic for several years. After the establishment of the Great Zhou Dynasty, thanks to Your Majesty's wisdom, the chaotic period has been shortened and the scope reduced. I hope that in the remaining years of my life, I will be able to witness a prosperity surpassing that of the Zhen Guan period of Emperor Taizong!"

Wu Zhao smiled. Her life seemed like a ship that had weathered the storm and and returned into a safe harbor, in need of serenity.

Dee Renchieh's wish was in line with hers, and she slowly asked Wan'er to bring a copy of the imperial edict. After reading it, she handed it to Dee Renchieh.

The edict was to bestow death upon Lai Chünchen.

"Your Majesty..." Dee Renchieh stood up uneasily from the brocade stool, holding a scroll in his hands.

"This morning I have sent for the execution, and the death of Lai Chünchen signifies the end of the past way of ruling. " She said calmly, and retrieved the copy of the edict and handed it back to Wan'er.

"Your Majesty, executing Lai Chünchen at this time may lead to mess among his subordinates!" Dee Renchieh clearly expressed his concerns.

"No, it won't." The Empress said firmly, "I have made arrangements long ago, nothing will go wrong. I am fully confident in ending the past, as for the future development, I dare not say now. Renchieh, I hope you can help me shoulder some of the burden."

"Your Majesty, I will do everything I can." Dee Renchieh replied, bowing.

"Renchieh, I hope to have more leisure time in the future." the Empress smiled slightly, "I should also enjoy myself. In fact, I used to enjoy myself - if I didn't separate public and private matters, and adjust myself, I wouldn't have been able to hold on for so long." She paused slightly, "Renchieh, from the Ming Hall to the Mirror Hall, my private life has been eventful as well."

"Your Majesty, I have heard that..."

"Do you know the Mirror Hall?" The Empress suddenly smiled, "What have you heard people say about it?"

"Well," Dee Renchieh interjected awkwardly, "people criticize Your Majesty's indulgence."

"In my view, a monarch's leisure pursuits within the bounds of non-neglecting official duties is justifiable. What do you think?"

"Yes, Your Majesty." Dee Renchieh replied in a somewhat awkward manner, unsure of the implication of the Mirror Hall, and continued, "As the supreme ruler, personal indulgence is certainly beyond reproach."

"Renchieh..." Wu Zhao suddenly had a strange idea - she had heard rumors more than once... People said that she had an ambiguous relationship with Dee Renchieh.

At this moment, she looked carefully at Renchieh. He was old, but his dignified and resolute demeanor still remained. She thought to herself: such a man is indeed worthy of love. However, she understood that she could not love him, and he would not accept her love. There is an insurmountable boundary between friends and lovers. Nevertheless, in a fleeting moment of reverie, she thought of taking this friend to see the Mirror Hall. So she stood up and said, "Earlier I mentioned the Mirror Hall to you. It is a miracle in architectural engineering that has never appeared in our history."

As Renchieh hesitated, the Empress gestured to Wan'er and then continued:

"I'll take you to see this miraculous hall."

She was not trying to replace the Zhang brothers with Dee Renchieh. It was an impulse that compelled her to showcase the splendor of the Mirror Hall. Apart from discussing its marvels with a few favorites such as the Zhang brothers, she had never talked to any of the high-ranking officials. But at this moment, she felt it wouldn't hurt to let Dee Renchieh see it.

Wan'er was surprised by the Empress's behavior, but she could see that the Empress was in a good mood, so she dared not defy or offer any advice. So they headed towards the magnificent Mirror Hall, a masterpiece on the earth.

The Mirror Hall was a place of brilliance and splendor. As Dee Renchieh walked in, he felt a sense of disorientation, calling out uneasily for the Empress.

The Empress looked at the gray-haired Dee Renchieh in the bronze mirror and asked with a peaceful smile, "How do you like this place?"

"Your Majesty..." Dee Renchieh's eyes were stimulated by the reflection of the mirror, and he replied with concentration, "This is a strange place, a strange and unprecedented place."

"Yes, this is unprecedented, this is a creation," she proudly interjected, "The Ming Hall of the past was the pinnacle of grandeur, while the Mirror Hall now was the pinnacle of magnificence."

"Magnificent to the extreme, yes, Your Majesty, my vision is failing here, I feel dazzled, I see all colors mixed together..." He almost gasped.

"Pull down the window." Wu Zhao ordered leisurely, wanting to show Dee Renchieh the night view of the Mirror Hall.

The windows were closed one by one, and the Mirror Hall was plunged into darkness. Dee Renchieh panicked, immediately thinking that any mishap in the darkness would lead to chaos. He tried to express his thoughts, but the sudden darkness prevented him from speaking. However, in the blink of an eye, he suddenly saw a light.

It seemed to be a cold light, and he was about to identify the source of this faint light when suddenly lanterns appeared everywhere! It was a candle, reflecting countless lanterns in the mirror, and soon all the candles around were lit.

Just now, the Mirror Hall was completely dark, but now it was dazzlingly bright. The sudden darkness and brightness made Dee Renchieh's eyes unable to adapt, so he closed his eyes, feeling his heart beating faster and faster.

"Renchieh, this is different from ordinary candle, isn't it?" the Empress asked cheerfully.

"Yes, yes," Dee Renchieh gasped, "This must be the ultimate light. However, Your Majesty, my body is weak, I feel dizzy in such an environment. I would like to request Your Majesty's permission to withdraw first."

Wu Zhao hesitated slightly, then smiled charmingly.

"Well, I won't keep you any longer." she said, as she ordered a maid to accompany Dee Renchieh out.

When Dee Renchieh left, the Empress laughed at having teased him - it was the mood of a big child, a combination of lightness and joy.

"Your Majesty," Wan'er looked at the Empress and asked in confusion, "Why did you bring him here? You used to say that we should keep public and private matters separate."

"There is no reason for this." Wu Zhao laughed, as if she wanted to dance with joy.

"Your Majesty, Minister Dee seems uneasy in this place."

"I appreciate his awkwardness," the Empress sighed, "I want to show him around and let him experience it. Their daily life is too restrictive. As long as he sees it a few more times, he won't be surprised anymore.Now..." she looked at the candlelight, thinking of summoning the Zhang brothers. But in an instant, the glare of the bronze mirror made her head spin, so she swallowed the words on the tip of her tongue.

"Now what?" Wan'er glanced at her.

If under normal lighting, Wan'er would definitely be able to see the Empress's pale face, but in the Mirror Hall, under the reflected light of the bronze mirror, the pale complexion caused by a moment of dizziness went unnoticed.

However, Wu Zhao herself was panicked by this dizziness. She felt palpitations during the dizziness, and a chill spread quickly from her spine to her limbs.

This was an unprecedented phenomenon, and Wu Zhao immediately thought of aging and death.

"Your Majesty!" Wan'er was surprised by the sudden silence of the Empress.

"I'll go back..." she said in a trembling voice, reaching out her hand to let Wan'er help her up.

When Wan'er touched the hand of the Empress, it was cold and sweaty.

Wu Zhao struggled with illness for twenty days, and then resumed her duties as usual.

Among the officials, very few knew that the Empress was ill. The Empress kept the news of her illness tightly sealed, to the extent that she did not summon physicians through the Imperial Medical Bureau. Zhang Yichih secretly brought two doctors into the Palace from the city center, with Shen Nanch'iu assisting in treatment. These three physicians were all housed in the Heavenly Palace.

Wu Chengsi and Wu Sansi knew that the Empress was ill, but they did not know the true condition of her. They only knew that the Empress had a minor illness like a cold. At the same time, they were also ordered not to disclose this information to outsiders.

In addition, Dee Renchieh, who was once invited to visit the Mirror Hall, also knew about the Empress's illness.

After visiting the Mirror Hall, Dee Renchieh was reinstated and replaced the former Li Zhaode as a prominent minister of the Great Zhou Dynasty.

Among all the officials, only he visits the Empress at the Heavenly Palace every other day.

After twenty days of struggle, the Empress recovered from her illness. She dressed up and attended the court as usual. On the third day following her recovery, she came to the Mirror Hall once more.

The reflection of the copper mirror once damaged her eyesight and caused her to feel palpitations and dizziness, but she did not recognize the connection. Occasionally, she would think about the relationship between her eyesight and the reflection of the copper mirror, but she denied it. She wanted to enjoy the splendor and brilliance of the mortal world at the Mirror Hall. Moreover, for an abnormal psychological reason, she felt that indulgence deserved to be cherished.

During the twenty days she spent in bed, she was deeply worried about aging. Going to the Mirror Hall was a way for her to use her psychological strength to resist physical aging. Her mental strength was so terrifyingly strong that she could work and enjoy herself even beyond her capacity.

Wan'er could see the Empress's aging and her struggle with aging, and sometimes she would secretly inform Princess Taiping of the Empress's situation.

Before long, the Zhang brothers also noticed the Empress's fatigue, and they began to worry about their own future. They had not yet established their own foundation, and the situation would be unimaginable once the Empress passed away.

As for Shen Nanch'iu, he gave the Empress stimulants regularly and in fixed quantities.

This was the life of the Empress. Two months later, the effects of that illness were considered resolved, but it was only a superficial resolution. After attending court every day, she tended to feel tired, even yawning in the court session.

One day, after morning court, she fell asleep in the sedan on her way back to the Heavenly Palace, and was awakened by Wan'er when she arrived.

This was something she had never experienced before. She hated her body. However, after entering the room, when Zhang Yichih was massaging her, she fell asleep again. Although she woke up immediately, she was still in a trance... ...

In a state of half-sleep, the Empress of the Great Zhou had a flowing dream. She seemed to be on the grass, at the edge of the sky, at the corner of the earth, and in the midst of void. Suddenly, she felt that her body had turned into a parrot, and the parrot was flying. Soon, there was a sound like thunder or lightning, and the parrot's wings were suddenly broken. She was shocked and screamed.

"Your Majesty..." Zhang Yichih called softly beside her.

She pressed her hands against her chest, groaning in pain...

"Your Majesty!" Zhang Yichih pulled her hand away and shook her again.

"Oh, Yichih, Yichih, I..." The Empress was still trembling with fear, holding onto him with both hands, "I had a terrible dream...so scary... Really, I was sweating all over... "

"Your Majesty, what kind of dream is it?"

"Ah, this..." She calmed herself down, took a breath, and said it again in a low voice.

"This dream..." Zhang Yichih felt puzzled, and a subtle association arose in his mind: the Empress's surname was Wu, so the parrot was undoubtedly the Empress herself; and the two broken wings made him think of his brothers, so he shuddered.

"My surname is Wu, a parrot, alas, that's me!" the Empress muttered to herself, "Broken wings, what does that signify?"

"Do you want somebody to come and interpret the dream for you?" Zhang Yichih asked anxiously.

The Empress did not respond immediately. In the past, she was strong and rarely showed reverence for the gods, thinking that human determination could overcome anything. However, recently, her physical strength has declined, and she could no longer ignore everything. Therefore, even a random dream has troubled her. Although she did not immediately summon someone in to interpret the dream, she was filled with doubts and turned over in her mind what the dream of a parrot with broken wings might imply.

"Will I never be able to fly again?" she asked herself silently, "If I can't fly, will I lose my power? Who shall snatch my power away?" These thoughts kept swirling in her mind, and she found it impossible to fall asleep again that night due to this dream.

The next day after the morning court session, she called her close ministers to stay and summoned them to another hall to ask them to interpret her dream.

The Empress's dream sparked some complex discussions, but these discussions were not directly aimed at the Empress of Great Zhou. She understood people's reservations and said:

"You can analyze it in detail, whether it's good or bad, just talk casually, after all, this is just a dream."

At this moment, Wei Sili, an attendant in the Imperial Secretariat, glanced at Wu Sansi and Wu Chengsi, and loudly spoke to the Empress:

"It might refer to these two men - the wings of the parrot, if not taken care of, will fall off. Moreover, in terms of kinship, these two are the closest to Your Majesty!"

The Empress nodded silently - this saying suggested an initial impulse for elevating one prince of the Wu clan as the Crown Prince. Since she became the Empress, people would mention it in front of her every now and then, sometimes praising the wisdom of Wu Sansi, sometimes extolling the virtue of Wu Chengsi... On these matters, she always remained silent, and up to now, the Crown Prince of Great Zhou was still Li Dan - a son of Li Chih. She had thought about making Wu Chengsi or Wu Sansi the Crown Prince, but these were just empty speculations.

Because the Empress rarely expressed her opinions on the matter of the Crown Prince, it was thought that the great revolution of the Great Zhou would see no continuity with the previous emperor's offspring. Therefore, those who seek to curry favor with the powerful set sights on Wu Sansi and Wu Chengsi. For many years, the most intriguing issue in the court has been the issue of instituting the Crown Prince.

"Anything else? About the dream?" the Empress asked gently.

"Your Majesty..." Cui Hsüanhui, an attendant of the Heavenly Palace, reported, "I believe this is a reaction to the weakening of the royal family back then, a reflection of Your Majesty's nostalgia for the past lingering in the dreams."

These words were straightforward and astonishing to everyone.

Wu Zhao was slightly shaken. She had once ruthlessly eliminated members of the Tang imperial family, two of whom were her sons - the late first Crown Prince Hong and the late second Crown Prince Hsien. She wondered... could the two wings refer to them? So, she asked again, "What else?"

"Your Majesty," Tian Guidao, the Minister of the Summer Palace, stepped forward and said, "What Minister Wei said just now is right. Past events are not worth troubling Your Majesty's mind."

This was another way out for the Wu brothers, and following him, two other people successively expressed the same opinion. The Empress remained silent, and she signaled with her eyes for people to continue speaking.

"Your Majesty, based on the dream, I dare to request to appoint a new Crown Prince..." Assistant Prime Minister Lu Zhifang said hesitantly.

"Minister Dee, what is your opinion..."

"Your Majesty, I am stupid." Dee Renchieh stepped forward in the dangerous situation. He said loudly, "In my humble opinion, the ones closest to Your Majesty are the current Crown Prince and Prince Luling. There is no closer relationship in the world than that between mother and children, and there is no one who can be compared to them. I hope Your Majesty will consider this. "

"Hmm..." the Empress responded in a drawn-out voice.

"Your Majesty, wings refer to children, hence the parrot without wings may be a hint that the Great Zhou is currently childless." Wang Chishan, the Left Deputy Prime Minister stood up and spoke for Wu Sansi again. He emphasized that the Great Zhou Dynasty had no heir, which was a crucial problem for a country. The Empress of the Great Zhou was surnamed Wu, while the Crown Prince and the Prince of Luling were both surnamed Li.

This seemed to force the Empress to make a decision. She looked at everyone and said in a serious tone:

"If you talk about sons, there remain two with me; I wish not to think upon this through dreams. If one were to guess what visions these might be in a dream, there will be a lot."

The debate about the Crown Prince came and went fruitlessly. Wu Zhao's dream never received a satisfactory answer, but she was unwilling to explore it further. She understood that delving deeper into politics would only lead to more trouble.

However, her dream gave rise to a number of rumors in the Palace. These rumors were multifaceted. Some said that the Empress would alienate the Wu clan, while others said that the Wu clan might unite to eliminate the remaining forces of the Imperial Li family. The so-called remnant forces of Imperial Li Family naturally refer to the Crown Prince and Prince Luling who had changed their surname to Wu.

The rumors troubled her a little bit and her energy had been declining rapidly in the past year. Before, she was just like an old woman, but now, she really was. Her skin was rough and loose, with more and more wrinkles, and her vision was getting more and more blurred. She felt that she could only see everything clearly in the Mirror Hall. For this reason, she was addicted to the Mirror Hall in which she spent most of the day...

One day, the Empress met Dee Renchieh in the Heavenly Palace and talked about the Mirror Hall again.

"Your Majesty," Dee Renchieh seemed to be chasing some thoughts from his memory, and said slowly, "this immortal place may be harmful to the body..."

"Harmful to the body?"

"Yes, the changing light there, the breathtaking light, is harmful to the eyes, and I think it will harm the heart as well. Your Majesty, have you had any special feelings during these days?"

"Ah..." she exclaimed suddenly, "my heart, my heart... it was the mirror that deceived me! Renchieh..." she sighed, "it seems that even the best things have their flaws."

They talked like old friends, and gradually she realized that Dee Renchieh was also getting old.

"Renchieh, we are getting old!" she said without any pretense, and naturally used the word "we".

"Your Majesty's spirit is still the same as it was in previous years," Dee Renchieh felt a strange feeling about the word "we" and answered cautiously, "I am getting old, and I would like to request Your Majesty's permission to retire."

"Retire..." she said slowly, "I haven't yet, are you tired already?" She smiled, paused for a moment, and then continued thoughtfully, "These years can easily make people tired. Renchieh, logically, we should retire at our age, we have done quite a lot in our lifetime."

Dee Renchieh's heart skipped a beat as he silently assessed the Empress's words. These words were probably heartfelt, and he wanted to seize this opportunity to advise the Empress to abdicate. However, this was a huge issue, and he pondered what words to use as an opening statement. He thought to himself: if he said it and it didn't work, it would affect the effectiveness of future advice.

"Renchieh, I am also tired. I have been wanting to retire for a long time." She said leisurely and dreamily.

Dee Renchieh glanced at the Empress in surprise - he was thinking about something, but the Empress had already spoken it out. He thought: Is she really that smart?

"But!" she sighed softly, continuing, "I still can't help but worry. If I were to give up power, I don't know what changes might occur."

"Your Majesty, the Crown Prince is loyal and prudent..." Dee Renchieh stammered.

"My son is loyal and prudent," she said with a bitter smile, "but that's not the problem!" She paused for a moment and continued with a bitter smile, "If my son were as capable as I am, I wouldn't have to worry. Unfortunately, he is mediocre, foolish, and lacks intelligence. Such people are the most likely to cause trouble."

The Empress criticized the Crown Prince without reservation, leaving the loyal minister Dee Renchieh at a loss for words.

"Recently, I feel that Prince Luling is more kind than the Crown Prince." Wu Zhao muttered to herself. It was not something she should have expressed, but it slipped out unintentionally.

Of course, Dee Renchieh dared not speak up, so he lowered his head.

"Managing my family affairs is more difficult than managing state affairs," she sighed softly, "in fact, both Chengsi and Sansi are more capable than my two sons," she paused again, and continued with a sigh, "I don't understand why people oppose my nephew's succession."

"Your Majesty, that is the people's loyalty to Your Majesty." Dee Renchieh seized the opportunity and spoke with grave solemnity.

"Loyalty to me?"

"Your Majesty, people think about what will happen to your posterity. It is unique throughout history that only sons have consecrated temples and offered sacrifices for their parents. Never before has a nephew established a temple in honor of his aunt." Dee Renchieh spoke with utmost sincerity and straightforwardness.

Wu Zhao felt a tremor deep in her heart. She had never thought about the issue of sacrifice for eternity. She was practical and she had a clear understanding of current practical issues. Now, when Dee Renchieh mentioned issues after her death, the historical tradition seemed like a lost thing that has now been found again. She stared blankly at the old minister with gray hair and beard in front of her, feeling a mix of emotions and unable to speak for a moment.

"Your Majesty, forgive my ignorance, but may I ask if my words were inappropriate?" Dee Renchieh asked tactfully. Although phrased as a question, it actually served to reinforce his previous statement.

"Renchieh..." the Empress sighed softly, "You are right! We can change many things, but we cannot change tradition." She paused for a moment, then let out a heavy sigh, "Each clan has its own traditions, I understand..."

She spoke softly at the end, a voice that only she could hear, not audible to others.

However, Dee Renchieh was inspired by the tears in the shining eyes of the Empress, thinking to himself, "This unpredictable woman has finally succumbed to tradition. Tradition has led me to victory!" Seizing the opportunity, he did not want to linger, bowed respectfully, and said:

"I request to resign."

"Hmm." She choked back tears and replied, "Renchieh, you don't have to retire. Stay with me for a few more years!"

This was not an order given as a ruler, but a request made as a friend. They have crossed the boundaries of ruler and subject, they were already friends. Based on friendship, there was nothing that could not be discussed, and nothing that could not be requested.

Dee Renchieh agreed on the basis of friendship. He wanted to continue to serve the Empress in his current position until her death. He thought: "She and I are both old, and we won't live long."

Chapter 17

As twilight descended, the remaining light of the setting sun illuminated the tops of a row of pines in the imperial garden. With a gentle breeze, the branches swayed, and the lingering light of the fading sun also swayed.

A small palace carriage slowly approached along the path of white stones, crossed a small bridge, and arrived at the south gate of the Heavenly Palace.

The palace carriage went straight to the gate, where it was taken over by four chamberlains from the inner court who would push it forward.

Sitting in the carriage was Empress Wu Zhao of the Great Zhou.

The Empress smiled and gestured to stop the palace carriage. Then she whispered, "I want to get down and walk."

So, two chamberlains helped the Empress down from the carriage slowly. The Empress's steps were slow and labored as she ascended the steps.

It is the old age when everyone must pass through, for as nature's day has its declining sunsets, so too does man's life have its twilight years. Signs of old age are inevitable.

However, the attendants in the Heavenly Palace believed that the Empress's prostration was but a temporary state for she had indeed been unwell for three months! Now, she was just beginning to recover from a serious illness, not truly old... And the Empress herself believed this as well. She thought that in a few more days, she would regain her strength. In order to show that her physical strength was recovering, she decided to take a walk.

On the corridor of the southern hall of the Heavenly Palace, the lanterns have been lit. In the twilight of the setting sun, the light was dim, obviously not harmonizing with the color of the sunset. She glanced at it, furrowed her brows, but did not express any opinion.

Her maid, Lady Wan'er came forward to greet her, bowing respectfully.

"Your Majesty, all the courtiers of the Crane Bureau are waiting to greet you."

The Empress revealed a fresh smile and continued to walk inward.

So Zhang Yichich, the Supervisor of the Crane Bureau led a group of men including Zhang Changzong, Chi Hsü, Tian Guidao, Li Chiunghsiu, Hsüeh Chi, among others, to welcome the Empress. They cheered with the cry of "Long live the Empress!"

The curtains in the Southern Hall had already been lowered, and inside the hall, lanterns and candelabras burned brightly. The Empress smiled radiantly as she leisurely addressed Zhang Yichih:

"It was my first night banquet in three months."

"With Your Majesty's recovery, it will now be possible to entertain the courtiers at all times!" Zhang Yichih mechanically replied - usually, he was lively in front of the Empress, but tonight, he obviously showed a tendency of restraint and unease.

The Empress sat down on the soft couch in the hall and took a sip of water from the cup handed to her by Wan'er.

"Your Majesty, I have arranged for several guests to come!" Zhang Yichih reported hesitantly.

"Guests?" The Empress frowned in confusion, "Are they from the Southern Court?"

"They are the Crown Prince, the Prince of Hsiang, Princess Taiping, and the Princess Consort." Zhang Yichih replied mechanically.

"Hmm," Empress Wu glanced at him, surprised but not angry, and said lightly, "How can they be guests? It's my family banquet now."

"To celebrate Your Majesty's recovery, a family banquet is most fitting. Furthermore, since Prince Luling was summoned to succeed the throne, he has not yet had a banquet with Your Majesty." Zhang Yichih finally settled down and said calmly, "And the Prince of Hsiang also..."

"Then let them in."

Zhang Yichih looked at his younger brother Zhang Changzong, who bowed and took three steps back, turned around and ordered the chamberlains to open the door leading to the next room.

Princess Taiping entered first and knelt down in front of the Empress, affectionately calling out, "Mother, Your Majesty..." with a hint of childishness as before.

Next, the two sons of the Empress walked in, one after the other, and greeted the Empress nervously.

Three months after the dream interpretation, the Empress did something that was actually meaningless but favored by the elder and respected officials: The Prince of Luling who was stationed in Fangzhou was summoned back and reinstated as the Crown Prince. The original Crown Prince, Li Dan, was demoted to Prince of Hsiang. Both were her biological sons and should have been cherished by the elder and respected officials. However, when Emperor Gaozong passed away, Li Zhe was first appointed as the Crown Prince and then demoted to Prince of Luling, causing people to have inexplicable nostalgic feelings and sympathy for him, hoping for his restoration. The Empress considered this to be absurd and ignored it. However, Dee Renchieh advised her to compromise on this issue that had no practical significance. At the same time, Zhang Yichih and Zhang Changzong also made the same request to the Empress - they had been trying to establish a support network outside the court over the past year in order to ensure their own survival. Therefore, they often echoed Dee Renchieh on many matters by the Empress's side.

Thus, the Great Zhou Dynasty established a new power group with Dee Renchieh as the core. Dee Renchieh introduced a group of talented people, such as Su Weidao, Li Ch'iao, Zhang Chienchih, Yao Yuanchong, Huan Yanfan, Ching Hui, and many others. The people of

Luoyang exclaimed, "All the talents in the world are in Dee's group. " This faction, on one hand, pledged loyalty to the Empress, while also subtly suppressing the Wu Clan.

Over the past year, under the rule of the Dee Renchieh group, there has been a significant departure from the past harshness towards a wise and simple governance. The Empress seemed to be inclined towards transitioning from Legalism to Confucianism, not only tolerating but also encouraging Dee Renchieh to do so. During this year, the Great Zhou Dynasty has been stable and peaceful, and the banquet tonight, which Zhang Yichih dares to invite the Crown Prince and the Prince of Hsiang to attend, was also a result of the benevolent governance in the past year.

The Empress looked at her two sons and suddenly remembered the dream of the parrot with broken wings. She sighed softly and asked, "Are you two brothers in good health?"

"Thank you, Your Majesty, we are fine."

So the Empress gestured for them to sit down, then turned to ask Princess Taiping, "Why did you also come in secret, Ah Zhu?"

"I am accompanying my husband to come and don't mean to surprise Your Majesty." She said, prompting her husband, Wu Youchi, to step forward and bow.

The Empress looked at the husband of the Princess with a different kind of emotion - he was a member of the Wu family, and he was the only one belonging to the Wu family at the banquet tonight. She suddenly felt that the Zhang brothers and the Wu family seemed unable to get along peacefully. Then she remembered the death of Wu Chengsi, which happened three months ago. She received the news of his death while lying in bed, and at that time, she was filled with deep sorrow. It was not because of Chengsi's death itself, but because she was shocked by the decline of the family in the same generation, reflecting her own old age. Although that emotion has now subsided, she couldn't help but feel that the Wu family was not as powerful as the Li family in various aspects when she saw Wu Youchi. With this thought in mind, she looked at Wan'er and slowly said:

"Today we have the family banquet, send for Sansi as well."

Before the banquet began, the chamberlains first presented snacks and wine, while four acrobats performed in the hall. Then the Zhezhi dance performance was presented. The banquet officially started when Wu Sansi arrived.

When Wu Sansi entered, he brought some unfortunate news to the Empress in a hushed tone.

"Your Majesty, Dee Renchieh's condition has worsened this afternoon and his life is in danger."

The Empress was shocked, but in an instant, she calmed down and said gently:

"There is no need to disclose this information now. He's in good health, I believe he will recover." She said, then turned to Wan'er, still lowering her voice, "Send the Deputy Chief of the Imperial Medical Department with two physicians to examine Dee Renchieh. I heard he is seriously ill." She paused for a moment and added, "He has been sick for only a few days!"

"Yes, today seems to be the ninth day of his being bedridden."

"Well, I hope he will be fine. Losing such an assistant is very unfortunate for me!" The Empress suppressed her emotions and continued quietly, "Wan'er, inform the Deputy Chief of the Imperial Medical Department to bring some chamberlains and report to me if there is any incident."

The Empress's mood changed due to the news of Dee Renchieh's illness. She was strong, but her weak emotions on the brink of life and death made her cherish every moment.

She looked around at the people in front of her - her son, daughter, son-in-law, nephew, and her lovers, all gathered together, seeming harmonious and warm. However, when one is vulnerable, there is a sense of impermanence. She thought to herself, "How long can such a gathering last?" She also thought, "Time changes with circumstances, if I were to die like Wu Chengsi, or fall seriously ill like Dee Renchieh, would these people still be able to get along so harmoniously as they are now?"

This kind of emotional burden was something she had never experienced before, but at this moment, one thing after another entered her mind, and she frowned from time to time...

"Your Majesty, is there anything that displeases you?" Zhang Changzong leaned in and asked softly.

"Nothing!" Her voice was low and weak, and dragged on for a long time, while her gaze lingered on Zhang Changzong's face.

Zhang Changzong was in the prime of his life with fresh and tender cheeks. Wu Zhao thought of the daily gossip of the courtiers in the Crane Bureau:

"Changzong's face resembles a lotus flower!"

"A lotus flower resembles Changzong's face!"

The first sentence compared Zhang Changzong to a lotus flower, implying that he was not as good as a lotus flower; however, the second sentence compared the lotus flower to Zhang Changzong, suggesting that the lotus flower was not as good as him.

In a dreamlike state, the Empress reached out her hand and caressed Zhang Changzong's cheek, as she spoke gently:

"A lotus flower resembles Changzong's face!"

"Your Majesty." Zhang Changzong's cheeks flushed slightly as he whispered softly, a subtle reminder that he should not be too presumptuous in front of the Empress's children.

However, Wu Zhao was bold and fearless; over the years, she has ignored her age and openly displayed her relationship with her lovers without any concealment. Back then, she opened the Mirror Hall to Dee Renchieh with such a mindset.

"Changzong's face resembles a lotus flower!" The Empress's hands continued to move, "Both are good..."

She was in a state of drifting, but even at that moment, the feeling of impermanence would also invade her. She thought that after she grew old and died, Changzong, who had a face as pretty as a lotus flower, would also drift away.

With a sudden impulse, she picked up the chopsticks and tapped on the copper plate.

With a loud bang, all eyes at the banquet turned to the Empress, and the musicians' performance came to a sudden halt.

The Empress whispered to Wan'er, instructing the musicians and performers to withdraw.

This was the prelude to a big announcement, and everyone waited in silence.

Suddenly, the whole hall fell silent.

"I am old!" The Empress continued solemnly, "My hope lies with you, I hope that in the future - you will all be well." She paused, and continued slowly but firmly, "Unity and mutual assistance are the conditions for survival."

So, led by the Crown Prince Li Zhe, the crowd stood beside the Empress, while Zhang Yichih and Zhang Changzong remained by her side. This was because they were not members of the royal family. However, Wu Zhao made a gesture, instructing them to line up in front of her.

"The banquet tonight is accidental, but I hope that good times can last forever..." The Empress paused, and then continued, "I want you all to become brothers and sisters and swear to heaven and earth before me! In the future, may you share both blessings and misfortunes. "

The crowd bowed to the Empress, then turned around, kowtowed to the sky, and silently prayed.

"Have a drink together!" The Empress said happily.

The crowd toasted the Empress for her longevity with the first cup of wine, and toasted each other with the second cup of wine.

This was an unwritten ritual, but Wu Zhao felt comforted by it. She thought that this ritual could guarantee future reconciliation.

Smart people could sometimes do childish and stupid things, and Wu Zhao was no exception. She was a politician who understood various political strategies and knew that politics was all about interests without morality. However, at this moment, she felt excited and comforted by the oath of the people in front of her to share weal and woe, and she thought it would be reliable. The declared fraternal vow in public would guarantee the unity and coexistence of the next generation.

So, in her excitement, she filled a cup of wine and drank it off with her sons and daughter, nephews and lovers. She looked relieved and said to everyone slowly: "Our hard days are over. From now on, as long as we stay on track, there will be no more trouble. "

"Long live the Empress!" Wu Sansi held the wine cup and bowed down.

The crowd followed him, shouted "Long live the Empress!" and drank heartily.

Wan'er quietly instructed the chamberlains to summon the music band and play the grand music.

It was the music played during the celebration, with a majestic and uplifting tune. The Empress's cheeks were flushed with wine, but when the music started, she sat upright and enjoyed the great melody.

Now, she thought it was the peak stage of her life. Both internal and external issues have been resolved one by one. After experiencing a rough road, she was now on a smooth path. Now she saw the future clearly! The future was shining brightly.

The grand music ended, and the Empress handed a cup of wine to Wan'er in appreciation for her long-term service as a court lady. She then ordered rewards for the musicians and singers.

Just at this moment of great excitement, the Chief of Imperial Residence and the Deputy Chief of the Imperial Medical Department both came to pay their respects, and reported:

"Dee Renchieh, the Prime Minister and Minister of the Central Secretariat, passed away due to illness."

The Empress stared blankly at the Chief of Imperial Residence. The excitement and joy just now made her forget about the critically-ill Dee Renchieh. Now that the news of his death had arrived, she was puzzled and surprised, and for a moment didn't know how to react.

The Deputy Chief of the Imperial Medical Department again reported to the Empress about the situation of Dee Renchieh.

"The last words of Minister Dee..." the Empress asked in a sorrowful and desolate tone.

"Minister Dee's last memorial will be presented by his son Dee Guangsi, the Vice Minister of Land. His last words were recorded by the attendant." The Deputy Chief of the Imperial Medical Department continued solemnly, "When Minister Dee was dying, he kept repeating 'May the country be peaceful and prosperous, and the Empress be healthy and happy', and nothing else was heard."

"Hmm." Wu Zhao woke up from her astonishment and confusion, tears welling up in her eyes as she mourned the passing of the old man. She said heavily, "Alas, the heaven snatched away one of my best ministers. I had hoped Renchieh would live a few more years, never thinking he would leave before me." Her voice choked up, in her personal thoughts, she wished Dee Renchieh was still alive, so that when she reached the end of her years, she could entrust him with her affairs.

Unexpectedly, Dee Renchieh, although younger than her, passed away first. Her feelings were complex at this moment.

Similarly, the Zhang brothers also felt a sense of emptiness. Over the past year, they have formed a bond with Dee Renchieh, relying on him as an external support. They pinned their hopes for the future on Dee Renchieh, but now the hope has been dashed.

"Cancel the banquet! Withdraw the music!" the Empress said gloomily.

The night banquet in the southern hall of the Heavenly Palace was dispersed.

When the Empress returned to the Changsheng Hall, she was exhausted and collapsed on the bed with her clothes on, as if asleep. Wan'er only took off the Empress's shoes and stayed by her side.

Before long, the Zhang brothers entered. Wan'er made a gesture for them to step outside the curtain, and followed them out, whispering, "Let Her Majesty rest! The passing of Minister Dee has greatly saddened her..."

"Oh!" Zhang Yichih pondered, "There may be changes in the court, I wonder who will take over Minister Dee's position."

"It's hard to say now..."

"Wan'er, at today's banquet, Her Majesty forgot to invite a few other people when she called us to take the oath. I think they will be jealous and resentful..." Zhang Yichih sighed softly, "Chi Hsü, Tian Guidao, they will definitely be unhappy with us brothers."

"They should not be dissatisfied - the Empress's statement today made it clear about your identities, how can Chi Hsü and the others participate in the oath ceremony?"

Zhang Yichih sighed softly and did not express any further opinions. The three of them sat by the incense cage outside the curtain to rest. Four palace maids were responsible for keeping watch inside and outside the curtain. Soon, the Empress summoned Wan'er to her bedchamber.

The Empress had put on her nightgown and ordered Wan'er to sleep beside her.

"They are still waiting outside to serve Your Majesty," when Wan'er mentioned "they," she was referring to Zhang Yichih and Zhang Changzong.

"Tell them to rest. It's getting late."

In the inner chamber, the scent of incense lingered in the air, and the sound of dripping water from the copper kettle was clear and faint. Although the Empress was very tired, she could not fall asleep. She spoke intermittently to Wan'er, all about the late Dee Renchieh.

"Wan'er..." she sighed softly, "Perhaps you know my personal feeling towards Renchieh!"

"I guess Her Majesty is secretly pleased with him, but he is unwilling to overstep the boundaries of friendship." Wan'er replied cleverly.

"Right." Wu Zhao sighed again, "Do you think he will know what's on my mind? Judging from his usual attitude, what do you think..."

"Your Majesty, Dee Renchieh is not foolish."

The Empress sighed deeply and said no more.

The long night dragged on, and the footsteps of the chamberlains patrolling the Palace grounds could be heard even in the inner chamber.

"Your Majesty, take a rest." Wan'er said softly.

The Empress yawned, seeming like she wanted to sleep, but then she started talking,

"Wan'er, what do you think would be a good posthumous title for Renchieh?"

"I think we should consult with the court officials and have Zhang Chienchih and Yao Yuanchong draft it."

"I don't want to borrow these people's hands." She approached the matter from a personal perspective.

"Your Majesty..." Wan'er called out softly, as if lamenting the Empress's tenderness towards the deceased.

Both of them closed their eyes with gentle hearts, seeming to rest and fall asleep. The sound of the dripping copper pot seemed to intensify, as if urging the long night to pass quickly or urging life to move towards its ultimate destination.

In the Palace, everyone was accustomed to the dripping of the copper kettle, but tonight, the Empress found the sound disturbing. She was restless, and she even thought of getting up to smash the copper kettle.

This was a vigorous thought, but she became drowsy in her restlessness - illusions entered her hazy consciousness one after another.

She saw Dee Renchieh walking towards her with his robe fluttering. Although Dee Renchieh was old, he was not feeble. He walked steadily, healthily, and even lovably.

She called out in a daze: "Renchieh..."

She was awakened by the sound of her own voice.

And she sighed, for the deceased friend, and for herself.

The copper kettle had leaked dry, and a maid promptly turned open the second copper kettle - outside, the sound of a drum was heard.

The Empress slowly sat up, "Wan'er! Let's go and see..."

Wan'er rubbed her eyes and looked blankly at the Empress.

"It's getting late now. If we don't hurry to Renchieh's house, it might be dawn soon." Wu Zhao said as she got off the bed and ordered the maids to fetch water and help her with her makeup.

The Empress spent more and more time on her makeup. Now, it would take her more than an hour to do it in the morning. She would first use a piece of white jade dipped in moist pearl powder and gently rub the skin on her face. Then she would apply dry powder and rouge, draw the eyebrows, and apply lip color, relying on these to cover up the wrinkles on her face.

She was careful and patient in doing makeup, spending her life on it...

In the faint light of dawn, the Left and Right Golden-Armoured Guards led the cavalry and ceremonial guards to clear the way, while two hundred Imperial Guards escorted the Empress as she left the Palace and headed towards the residence of the Prime Minister Dee Renchieh.

The Empress went to fulfill her final wish.

In her lifetime, she discovered many talented individuals, who rose to high positions, but only Dee Renchieh had a true friendship with her, and only he had entered the Mirror Hall among all the court officials.

On that day, the Empress posthumously awarded the late Prime Minister Dee Renchieh the title of Right Wenchang (Intellect Star) Minister and also conferred him the posthumous name of Wenhui (Intellect Grace).

On the same day, the Empress issued a special decree at the Heavenly Palace to close the Mirror Hall, a masterpiece of human ingenuity. This was done in memory of Dee Renchieh. She remembered that Dee Renchieh had once talked about the drawbacks of the Mirror Hall.

The history of the Great Zhou Dynasty came to a pause when Dee Renchieh passed away, and the peace he had created soon vanished.

Chapter 18

People say that when elderly people undergo temperament change, it is a sign of impending death.

The Empress's health was good, but her temperament has changed significantly. She was irritable and no longer as patient as before. She no longer maintained her former precision and rigor.

That was one year after the death of Dee Renchieh.

In the court, the people introduced by Dee Renchieh in the past, as well as those personally selected by the Empress, gradually formed a group opposing the Zhang brothers.

This group of people traditionally opposed a woman becoming the emperor, and they also traditionally believed that the emperor should come from the Li family. They received the stipend and hold titles from the Zhou dynasty, yet they claim to be loyal to the Tang emperors.

In the past, the struggle of this group was against the Wu clan and other newly emerging clans. Now they have changed their strategy and hope to break down the core figures of the Empress one by one, starting with targeting Zhang Yichih and Zhang Changzong.

Wei Yuanzhong, who was promoted from the Assistant Minister of Justice to the Assistant Prime Minister, joined forces with two attendants in the Imperial Secretariat Zhang Shuo and Song Ching, Assistant Imperial Censor Zhang Tinggui, Left Historiographer Liu Zhichi, the Chief Imperial Counselor Zhu Chingze, and the one in charge of the Ministry of Rites, Gao Chien, to become the vanguard against the Zhang brothers.

Yichih's another younger brother, Zhang Changch'i, was transferred from the position of Governor of Ch'izhou to the Governor of Yongzhou, but was vetoed by Wei Yuanzhong using his power.

In the court, they openly referred to the Zhang brothers as the "Two Young Boys". They also threatened that once the Crown Prince ascended the throne, the "Two Young Boys" would be the first to be executed.

The Empress also heard about it. She was enraged and resentful, deeming it an affront to her dignity and a challenge to her authority. In the past, she might have tried to reconcile, but at this moment, she could not tolerate it. She immediately imprisoned Wei Yuanzhong and Gao Chien, using her imperial authority to protect the Zhang brothers. Furthermore, she was also regretful, thinking that the oath they made a year ago had been abandoned by the Crown Prince - she believed that Wei Yuanzhong and his associates were connected to the Crown Prince.

As a result, with the support of the Empress, the Zhang brothers accused Wei Yuanzhong of plotting treason.

When the Empress personally interrogated, it naturally would not lead to a conclusion, but only deepen the contradictions. Those who were against the Zhang brothers' group took advantage of the trial to testify and severely criticize Zhang Yichih and Zhang Changzong, which angered the Empress. She no longer followed the formalities of the interrogation and used her power to demote Wei Yuanzhong to a low rank and exiled Zhang Shuo and Gao Chien to Lingnan.

This was the first time that Wu Zhao formally violated the law after becoming the Empress. In the past, she would have gone through legal procedures in any case.

However, such pressure did not quell the anti-Zhang wave. When Wei Yuanzhong resigned from the court and was exiled, he still resolutely reported:

"I am already old, and now I am heading to Lingnan, knowing that I have a narrow escape from death. However, I believe that Your Majesty will think about my words in the future." He paused, turned around and pointed at the Zhang brothers," These two young boys will definitely cause trouble in the future. "

Wu Zhao's expression changed, and she sternly ordered, "Leave!" Then she got up from the throne and led Zhang Yichih and Changzong out of the court.

Afterwards, the Empress granted some power to her lovers.

In the past, she wielded great power, even during the heyday of Lai Chünchen, he did not have independent power. He could exercise power only after reporting to the Empress and receiving authorization; as for Dee Renchieh, he obtained the power of the Empress to act at her own discretion under principles - it was like she gave someone a sword, but the handle of the sword was still in her own hand.

However, the power given to the Zhang brothers was different from the past. Now, she also handed over the hilt of the sword to her lovers.

This delivery, far from being rational, was prompted by emotion. When Zhang Changzong wept upon embracing the Empress's ankle and recounting his perilous situation, the Empress was moved by his tenderness and allowed them to introduce those close to them in court, thus fostering their factions. She also tolerated their dismissal of rivals.

Wan'er, a court lady who had served the Empress for many years, was surprised by this measure and thought to herself: Has the Empress changed her temperament?

On a sunny autumn afternoon, the grass turned yellow, and the leaves fell off the trees. The weather was nice, with a cool breeze invigorating the spirit. The autumn sun also gave a soft and gentle feeling.

Zhang Yichih and Zhang Changzong accompanied the Empress to bask in the sun on the grass in the courtyard of the Heavenly Palace.

The Empress had a habit of taking a nap, and she fell asleep under the warm sun.

The Zhang brothers were playing chess by the sleeping Empress. Soon, a chamberlain approached them quietly. Zhang Yichih glanced at the Empress, made a gesture, stood up, and walked to the artificial hillside nearly 20 meters away from the Empress. He whispered,

"Sha Ming, what information have you gathered?"

"I have received a special message," said the chamberlain named Sha Ming with a nervous expression in a low voice, "Prince Chiwei and the Empress's grandson Chongrun have joined forces to deal with you two. Their first step will be to overthrow Wu Yizong. "

"The first step is to overthrow Wu Yizong?" Zhang Yichih's eyes widened in surprise, "Sha Ming, your information may be incorrect. Prince Chiwei Wu Yanchi and Prince He'nei Wu Yizong are cousins. Some people are plotting against the Wu family. How could they turn against each other?"

Sha Ming shook his head, "Yichih, I haven't finished yet. Prince He'nei Wu Yizong led the troops to battle, recommended by you brothers, and he is very close to you, while Prince Chiwei has different thoughts. To be honest, Prince Chiwei has long-term plans in mind. He thinks that our Empress doesn't have many years left to live well, so he has already started to show favor to the Crown Prince for the future..."

"Oh, this is absurd. The Empress is in very good health; why will anyone think of her death?"

"It is a fact that Prince Chiwei is indeed heading down this path. I dare not say whether he has direct contact with the Crown Prince, but the Empress's grandson Chongrun and Prince Chiwei have been in frequent interactions. They definitely planned to overthrow Wu Yizong first, that is for sure, and within two or three days, they will definitely take some action."

Zhang Yichih furrowed his brows, pondered for a while, and then asked again:

"Have you heard anything about the conspiracy between the Empress's grandson and the Prince Chiwei?"

"It's hard to say," Sha Ming said solemnly, "they must have their own supporters, but their interactions are hard to detect by outsiders. The Princess Yongtai, younger sister of Chongrun, married Prince Chiwei, and all their communications are handled via Princess Yongtai."

Zhang Yichih fell into silence.

At the same time, Princess Taiping entered the grassland from another direction, without being noticed by Zhang Yichih and Sha Ming.

"Your Majesty, Changzong!" Princess Taiping walked up to the Empress and Zhang Changzong.

"Princess..." Zhang Changzong was surprised and stood up, bowing.

The Empress raised her eyelids slightly and saw her daughter in a daze.

"Mom!" Princess Taiping called out lightly, approaching the Empress. She said eagerly, "I've been waiting for a long time. Where is Wan'er? I was waiting for her to inform you, but since she didn't show up, I came on my own."

The Empress stretched her limbs and yawned.

"I should wake up now, sleeping for a moment is so comfortable!"

At this moment, Zhang Changzong held a white jade pot and a spittoon, serving the Empress to rinse her mouth. Zhang Yichih also noticed this and sent away Sha Ming before returning.

Wu Zhao saw Sha Ming walking out while she was rinsing her mouth, and she also saw Zhang Yichih walking towards her. Her eyesight had deteriorated, and she could only see a blurry figure walking away, barely able to make out that it was a chamberlain. So, she casually asked, "Who came to report?"

Zhang Yichih felt a bit embarrassed and said awkwardly, "It's Sha Ming..."

At this moment, Wan'er appeared from behind the rockery and walked slowly towards the Empress. When Princess Taiping saw her from a distance, she called out:

"Wan'er, where did you hide?"

Although Wu Zhao was still in a daze upon waking up, she had already sensed that something was going on between Zhang Yichih, Sha Ming, and Wan'er.

Two hours later, having sent away Princess Taiping and the Zhang brothers, Wu Zhao asked and Wan'er answered, "I overheard Yichih and Sha Ming talking behind the rockery! It's a matter of great importance, and I can't just barge in, but I feel like I should listen." Wan'er then detailed the conversation between Zhang Yichih and Sha Ming to Wu Zhao.

Wu Zhao raised her eyebrows and asked heavily:

"You didn't hear wrong? Wu Yanchi colluded with Chongrun?"

"Your Majesty, I believe I did not hear wrong."

"Um!" The Empress sighed through gritted teeth. She could not tolerate the Wu family members plotting against her, and at this moment, her hands were shaking slightly due to anger. Wan'er saw a blue glow on the Empress's cheek, which was murderous intent. In recent years, the Empress has become more benevolent and seldom showed murderous intent. However, the cruelty that had disappeared for a long time has now resurfaced.

Wan'er shuddered.

"Call in the Zhang brothers." she said slowly.

Princess Taiping was still lingering in the Palace, playing with her mother's two lovers. When Wan'er summoned the Zhang brothers inside, she asked softly:

"Wan'er, it looks like something is happening in the Palace?"

"Something happened, you'd better go back!" Wan'er smiled bitterly, "We just had a period of peace, and now there's trouble again."

Princess Taiping has always been cautious in dealing with her mother. She understood her mother's personality well, knowing that any overstep would bring bad luck upon herself. Therefore, she dared not inquire about the truth and hurriedly went back.

When Wan'er entered the inner room, the Empress and her two lovers were silently facing each other. Zhang Yichih lowered his head, expressionless, while Zhang Changzong knelt beside the Empress's knees.

"Wan'er," Wu Zhao called out coldly, "Sha Ming, the supervisor of the Heavenly Palace should be sentenced to death! "

The announcement sent shivers down the Zhang brothers' spines, and their gazes simultaneously fell on the unpredictable Empress's face.

"I don't allow chamberlains to do such things." She said to her lovers in a gentler tone.

"Your Majesty..." Zhang Yichih knelt down in fear, "That was my fault..."

"I know, I won't hold it against you," she sighed, "You should have someone do things for you, but I can't allow my people to violate my laws."

"Your Majesty, we have no intention of harming anyone, we just want to know more for our own safety. " Zhang Changzong said tactfully.

"I know, I will protect you," she said, sighing again, "as for the Chongrun siblings, I'll leave them to you to judge."

"Your Majesty, I think we should just let it go. If we investigate further, many people will be involved." Zhang Changzong said.

"No, I will not compromise." the Empress continued firmly, "Rest assured, I will not let anyone harm any of you. Don't mention it again."

The incident did not break out until after the morning court session on the third day.

Wu Zhao confirmed on the other hand the secret plot of Chongrun and Wu Yanchi against the Zhang brothers, as well as against Wu Yizong who followed the Zhang brothers.

She summoned the Chongrun siblings to the Palace for interrogation by Zhang Yichih and Zhang Changzong.

The young prince Chongrun ignored the feelings of an old woman towards her lovers, thinking that as a prince, he would always be superior to the Zhang brothers. Therefore, at the beginning of the interrogation, he sternly rebuked:

"You two are trying to sow discord between me and my grandma, hmph!" he said, then turned to bow to the Empress and said, "Your Majesty, your grandson has done nothing wrong."

The Empress slammed the imperial table grimly and scolded:

"You dare to be rampant in front of me. "

Princess Yongtai saw that something was not right and quickly said:

"Your Majesty, Chongrun was wrongly accused and he is unwilling to accept it, so he spoke rudely. "

"Are you conspiring to overthrow Wu Yizong? Is this accusation unjust against you?" the Empress said coldly, "Wu Yanchi has confessed. Is this unjust?"

"Wu Yanchi has confessed!" This statement shocked the Chongrun siblings. They were inexperienced and couldn't distinguish the truth in a hurry, so they were at a loss, while Wu Zhao sneered at them.

Princess Yongtai felt guilty, thinking that since the truth had been exposed, the only way out was to seek self-preservation. So she blurted out hastily:

"Your Majesty, I haven't heard of it."

"Don't you know they are trying to overthrow Wu Yizong?"

"Your Majesty, I'm completely unaware."

"Chongrun, your sister doesn't admit that she has sent messages for you." The Empress said casually.

Chongrun's face flushed red and he was unable to utter a word.

"What? Are you siblings really so heartless? Once the truth is revealed, you only care about clearing your own names and disregard your siblings?" Wu Zhao coldly smiled and made a gesture to the chamberlain on duty beside her.

Chongrun was so angry at his sister's lack of loyalty that he trembled and said,

"Your Majesty, the situation is like this: Wu Yizong conspired with the Zhang brothers to cause chaos. Yanchi and I discussed how to eliminate the threat, but we did not dare to do anything else. As for my sister, she had not heard of this matter in advance. "

The Empress did not say anything more, but the chamberlain on duty had already called four chamberlains to escort Chongrun and Princess Yongtai out.

According to the rules, the punishment was thirty strokes of the cane.

The chamberlains in charge of the cane punishment were biased towards the Zhang brothers. Naturally, they could see that this matter pertained to the Zhang brothers. Therefore, when executing the cane punishment, they put extra force into it. By the time Zhang Changzong pleaded with the Empress for the Chongrun siblings, they had been given twenty strokes of the cane.

After receiving twenty strokes, the two noble figures were unconscious and unable to move.

The Empress showed no mercy. She sternly ordered the two to be carried back to the Crown Prince's mansion. Then, she grimly commanded Zhang Yichi to draft an edict to sentence Prince Chiwei Wu Yanchi to death.

After taking these measures, the Empress returned to the Heavenly Palace in a melancholy mood, without accompanying the Zhang brothers.

The Zhang brothers achieved a complete victory in this round. However, after watching the Empress enter, they felt a sense of terror due to the severe punishment. Zhang Yichih sighed and said to his brother:

"Changzong, from now on, their grudge deepened."

"Let it go!" Zhang Changzong sighed helplessly.

"Changzong, the power of the royal family is strong," Zhang Yichih said dejectedly, "their enmity has grown so deeply that if the Empress were to suffer any misfortune in her later years, we would surely meet our doom."

"You're thinking too much," Zhang Changzong suddenly laughed wildly, "Think about those who served the Empress, how many of them had a good ending? Ming Chongyan and Hsüeh Huaiyi all met bad endings. We should anticipate our own fate."

"Changzong, the planning lies with man. If we can handle things well, seize power, or form a faction in the court with support, then the situation will be different." Zhang Yichih pondered, "Unfortunately, Chongrun turned against us. His father was reinstated as the Crown Prince mainly because of our advice to the Empress. Relying solely on Dee Renchieh is not easy to achieve our goals. Now, Chongrun has been severely punished, and it seems that our relationship with the Crown Prince is also broken."

Zhang Changzong did not speak again, slowly tidying up the documents.

At this time, a chamberlain came in to report that Prince Chongrun and Princess Yongtai had been beaten and sent back, but died on the way.

The two brothers looked at each other, and after a while, Zhang Yichih said dimly:

"Changzong, it looks like we also need to actively prepare. This struggle is not going to end peacefully."

Zhang Changzong responded calmly, then said solemnly: "We still have time."

Zhang Yichih, Minister of Guards and the Supervisor of Crane Bureau, gathered a group of literati and completed the compilation of a series of books, named "Masterpieces of Three Religions (Confucianism, Buddhism and Taoism) " which represented the literary achievements of the Great Zhou Dynasty.

On the day when "Masterpieces of Three Religions" was completed, Zhang Changzong, a Grand Master of the Palace with silver seal and blue ribbon, was granted the title of Duke of State of Ye.

These two matters were originally unrelated, but the Empress combined them together. It seemed that she transferred the credit for supporting "Masterpieces of Three Religions" from Zhang Yichih to Zhang Changzong.

In the court, "Masterpieces of Three Religions" did not receive special attention, but the title of Duke conferred upon Zhang Changzong attracted the attention of many people.

Since the death of Prince Chongrun, Prince Chiwei Wu Yanchi, and Princess Yongtai, the Zhang brothers' style has changed, with Zhang Yichih making efforts to collaborate with scholars and engage in the compilation of literary works.

Renowned poets such as Song Zhiwen, Shen Quanch'i, Du Shenyan, and others all attached themselves to the group of Zhang Yichih. Many young scholars in Luoyang also frequented Zhang Yichih's residence, regarding the Empress's lover as their master. In addition, talented officials such as Zheng Hsieh and Ran Zuyong, two assistant Imperial Censors, and Song Zhihsün, a Grand Master of the Palace, also became followers of Zhang Yichih.

As Zhang Yi was expanding his influence, Zhang Changzong seemed to have monopolized the position of the Empress's lover. He brought new joys to the aging Empress. Wu Zhao, no longer able to withstand the thrill of sexual pleasure due to her advancing age, needed a lover, someone masculine, but from a psychological perspective, she sought to negate her own decline. Zhang Changzong grasped onto this sentiment, making himself into a source of warmth, nourishing the Empress's soul.

There are some similarities between the elderly and children, so Wu Zhao naturally developed a childlike attachment to Zhang Changzong. When they were together, they would often talk endlessly about childish and funny folk myths. Sometimes, he would fall asleep in the Empress's arms, and likewise, the Empress would also fall asleep in his embrace.

Due to his proximity and the fact that he spent almost all his time with her, Zhang Changzong naturally came into contact with the political affairs. Like Wan'er, he assisted the Empress in handling state affairs and had access to many confidential documents.

The confidential documents were mostly related to the Zhang brothers. Zhang Changzong was very magnanimous. He never explained himself and never concealed people's attacks on him, as if it had nothing to do with him.

Wu Zhao appreciated his demeanor, and once she smiled and said to her lover:

"A true gentleman is magnanimous, and can face anyone without shame."

"Your Majesty, behind the gentle face, there are still uncomfortable feelings." Zhang Changzong lamented, "People always can't accept me, why is that?"

"I accept you!" The Empress laughed, tore up a memorial accusing the Zhang brothers, and threw it away.

The title of Duke of State of Ye was thus conferred. The Empress believed that the title could protect the status of her lover.

With his noble title and access to state secrets, Zhang Changzong naturally laid out his pawns for himself. Wei Chengch'ing, the Assistant Minister of Summer Palace, Cui Shench'ing, the Assistant Prime Minister, and Fang Rong, an Assistant Imperial Censor, all joined Zhang Changzong's group.

The establishment of any political group was always difficult, but the Zhang brothers managed to do it smoothly using their power, even winning over Yao Yuanchih, who had always been against them, and establishing connections with him.

The new group was quickly established and developed, but Zhang Changzong did not completely conceal it from the Empress and reported selectively. In his role as her lover, he spoke with youthful naivety:

"Now, when people come to beat me, I have helpers."

Wu Zhao has always prohibited her subjects from forming private alliances, but she did not restrain Zhang Changzong from forming his group. She replied to her lover:

"Is it not enough with me here?"

"You are not just a helper!" Zhang Changzong laughed and said, "You are the master, how can you be compared to a mere helper?"

"Well, having me is enough!"

"Sometimes, due to the overall situation, there are times when you have no choice..." Zhang Changzong murmured softly, "Your Majesty, I must admit, sometimes I am very scared."

The Empress suddenly gave birth to a maternal instinct, she looked at him for a long time - finally, she embraced Zhang Changzong and exclaimed excitedly:

"My child, rest assured, with me here, you will not be harmed in any way."

He nestled in the arms of the Empress and suddenly burst into tears, whether out of gratitude or affectation, his tears were like pearls hanging on his cheeks.

These two strings of pearl tears softened the heart of the Empress even more.

"Changzong," she wiped away tears for her lover and said gently, "Next year, I will let you select a group of people. If the conditions permit, I will appoint you as the Prime Minister."

"I don't want to be the Prime Minister!" Zhang Changzong said softly, "I would rather stay by Your Majesty's side. If Your Majesty is gracious enough to bestow the position of Prime Minister, then give it to Yichih. Besides, he is more capable than me in this aspect."

Wu Zhao touched his cheek, remaining silent for a long time. She was a wise woman and understood Zhang Changzong's intention to secure the position for his elder brother. However, out of love, she could not bear to regard this intention as a conspiracy. She thought to herself: they have the right to use strategy to protect themselves, don't they?

Zhang Changzong raised his head from the Empress's arms and asked leisurely:

"Your Majesty hasn't been to Chang'an for many years. Would you like to stay in Chang'an for a while?"

"Oh..." Wu Zhao's eyes shifted to the window. Chang'an, the former capital, was now overshadowed by Luoyang as the political center of the newly established Zhou Dynasty after the Tang Dynasty. Chang'an had become the western capital, visited only occasionally by her.

Now, when Zhang Changzong proposed a trip to Chang'an, she was moved. She contemplated the scenery on the Grand Road between Chang'an and Luoyang, and she also contemplated the magnificence and vastness of Chang'an. Compared to Luoyang, Chang'an was obviously more magnificent. However, she was getting older, and every time she traveled, it would involve a large number of troops and be extremely complicated. She was a little afraid of the hassle, but on the other hand, she felt that if she didn't go to Chang'an and stay for a year or two at this time, it would be difficult for her to move around when she got even older in the future. Therefore, she hesitated in this dilemma.

"If we get ready now, we can go in the spring next year, and return to Luoyang in the spring the year after." Zhang Changzong continued excitedly, "The finances of the dynasty are currently very abundant, and there is a surplus that Your Majesty can use. Let's make a three-year plan to travel between the two capitals."

"Oh!" Wu Zhao breathed a sigh of relief, "Speaking of finances, I have no regrets. During my years in governance, despite continuous external wars, the world was prosperous, surpassing the Zhenguan period of Emperor Taizong." Just then, Wan'er called out "Your Majesty" from outside the curtain, and Zhang Changzong stopped reciting a string of praises at his lips.

Wan'er came in and presented a special memorial.

"Prince Anping, Wu Youhsü resigned from his official position, retired to Mount Song, and left behind a memorial."

Wu Zhao was amazed and blurted out, asking:

"Has he left? Did he resign and leave a memorial?"

"Yes, Prince Anping explained in the memorial the reason for doing so, fearing that Your Majesty and relatives would keep him. If he did not abandon his position, he would not be able to refuse Your Majesty's retention, so he had to abandon his position and submit a memorial. Prince Anping also said that this was purely out of his nature and had nothing to do with political affairs." Wan'er said, handing over Wu Youhsü's memorial with both hands.

Wu Zhao's brows furrowed deeply as she glanced at the memorial and said,

"You keep it first; I'll take a closer look later."

The sudden report disrupted the Empress's good mood, and she did not believe in "retiring purely out of the nature". She thought that throughout history, there were always other reasons behind recluses. At the same time, she gained a concept from historical records that in times of peace, there were few recluses, but in times of chaos, recluses increased. She believed that encountering difficulties in official career or being forced into political situations would lead people to seclusion, but Wu Youhsü encountered no difficulties in his career, so it was only due to political reasons of a special kind that prompted him to retire.

What could be the reason? She couldn't guess.

In her imagination, the Wu family's prestige and prosperity had reached the extreme, and there was no reason for them to retreat.

In contemplation, she asked, "Why?"

Wan'er has already left the outdoors, and only Zhang Changzong was left by her side now.

The lover with a lotus-like face could not figure out why Wu Youhsü chose to retire, but he was quick-witted enough to handle it. When the Empress asked again "Why", he sighed and said:

"Your Majesty, Prince Anping is nobler than all of us."

Wu Zhao raised her eyes slightly and sighed softly:

"Not being obsessed with fame and fortune, although it can be considered noble, but this matter is not so simple. Talking about human nature, who does not envy wealth and glory?"

"Your Majesty, it is a good thing to have an aloof and proud person among a group of prosperous and prestigious people." Zhang Changzong said solemnly.

These words touched the Empress, and she smiled dreamily, saying:

"In the Wu family, there are many people vying for fame and fortune, but none is solitary and proud. That's right, Changzong, announce this matter." She said, seeming a little sad, "My clan finally has a man like Tao Yuanming[2]. "

Zhang Changzong used his intelligence to simplify the issue of Wu Youhsü abandoning his official position and retreating to the mountains, but this was not the reality. In fact, it was due to Wu Youhsü's despair towards the Wu clan ruling group that he decided to retire. From the death of the Prince Chongrun and Prince Chiwei, he saw that tragedies would continue to occur in the Empress's reign. At the same time, he also realized that this was an era without a future. Once the Empress died, it was unpredictable how the Wu clan would evolve. Therefore, he left to avoid the storm.

This was an omen, but the royal relatives in Luoyang were completely unaware of it and continued to struggle for power and fight each other.

The Empress was waiting anxiously for her lover Zhang Changzong on the Zetian Tower beside the Zichen Hall. Downstairs, the Assistant Minister of Justice and others were waiting for the Empress's orders.

There were several memorials on the Empress's desk. The court lady Wan'er stood nervously beside the Empress, glancing at the door curtain from time to time.

The atmosphere was eerie, and the eight chamberlains standing on either side of the door seemed afraid to even make a sound with their breath.

Two palace maids entered from the right side door and presented sweets to the Empress. She glanced at them and shook her head in refusal.

Just then, there was a report from outside the curtain:

"The Duke of State of Ye, Zhang Changzong, responded to the imperial decree."

The Empress took a deep breath, gestured to Wan'er, and then Wan'er summoned him in, while ordering the eight chamberlains in the curtain to leave.

Zhang Changzong has learned about the seriousness of the situation. He entered and knelt down in front of the Empress, anxiously saying:

"Your Majesty, spare me..."

The Empress's face was extremely solemn as she looked at her kneeling lover and asked sorrowfully:

"Is that true?"

Zhang Changzong raised his head in confusion and looked at the Empress.

"The Imperial Censorate has submitted three accusations to which the Prime Minister has attached a memorial, and Yang Yuansi from Xuzhou has reported your crime..."Wu Zhao's voice trembled, "Changzong, you are truly plotting treason."

"Your Majesty," Zhang Changzong was shocked, sweat beading on his forehead, and stammered, "How could I commit treason? How could I even think of committing treason? I beg Your Majesty to spare me, I am not guilty of treason."

"So, what is your crime?"

"The crime of being close to Your Majesty." Zhang Changzong said angrily, "I serve Your Majesty, but I have long been the target of public criticism. I have long anticipated that fists would be aimed at me. Some time ago, I asked Your Majesty to allow me to recommend a few people in the court, with support from outside, not to establish a faction, but to protect myself -Your Majesty, people hate me and will try every means to attack me..."

Wu Zhao paused for a moment and asked with a tone of regret:

"Yang Yuansi has confessed. Do you have any evidence? Did you say you were fit to be the emperor?"

Zhang Changzong shook his head in surprise.

"Your Majesty, I would not be so foolish."

"Yang Yuansi pointed out that you claimed to be the emperor, and Song Ching, the Assistant Minister of Justice, submitted a memorial to further confirm this point, with the testimony of the sorcerer Li Hongtai."

"Ah!" Zhang Changzong's heart pounded, and he shouted abruptly, "Those despicable scoundrels are conspiring to frame me, Li Hongtai, Li Hongtai..."

"Have you told him about the plan to become the emperor?"

"No, Your Majesty, it's not like that," Zhang Changzong's face turned red as he hurriedly said, "I have been worrying. Some time ago, when Your Majesty was slightly indisposed and did not attend court, it happened to be when I recommended Wei Chengch'ing to be appointed as the Prime Minister. There were rumors outside accusing me of plotting treason. I was panicked, and coincidentally someone introduced me to Li Hongtai, who is said to be good at fortune-telling.

I met with him a few times, and during one of our conversations, he mentioned that there would be a disaster soon, but it could be alleviated by building a Buddhist temple in Dingzhou. I thought that building a Buddhist temple couldn't be a bad thing, so I agreed. I also discussed with Li Hongtai about the construction details."

"Did you not say you wanted to become the emperor?"

"I did not say anything like that, it was Li Hongtai who said I have the appearance of an emperor. I thought he was joking and casually said: *If I were the emperor, you should be the Imperial Tutor*. Later, at a banquet, someone talked about physiognomy, and I also mentioned that people say I have the appearance of an emperor. Your Majesty, that's how it is, I did not lie."

"Changzong..." The Empress's expression gradually calmed down, and she said with sorrow, "You have been in the court for so long, how could you be so confused to end up in this situation? The words about being an emperor have solidified the accusation of your rebellion!"

"Your Majesty, how can I be the emperor? I am well aware of the taboos of the court, but I also understand the actual situation. Therefore, I find it ridiculous that the sorcerer flatters and talks nonsense, so I use it as a joke to tell." Zhang Changzong widened his eyes, "Your Majesty, does this constitute a crime of rebellion?"

"According to the law, yes."

"Your Majesty..." Zhang Changzong said anxiously, tears streaming down his face.

"Li Hongtai must have colluded with those people. It's possible that they framed you intentionally, but the law is impartial. This case can only be handed over for trial."

"Your Majesty, falling into their hands is like a sheep entering a tiger's den, with no hope of survival. Your Majesty once promised to protect me..."

"Hmm!" she pondered and said slowly, "I will handle this case together with Prime Minister Wei Chengch'ing, the Minister of Justice

Cui Shenqing, and the Assistant Minister of Justice Song Ching. Wei and Cui were both recommended by you, so they will not make things difficult for you. Just tell the truth as you said earlier."

"Your Majesty..." Zhang Changzong couldn't help but kneel down and said sorrowfully, "I beg Your Majesty to personally investigate. It's always unreliable in the hands of outsiders."

"Changzong!" The Empress said with a sigh, "Legal procedures cannot be ignored. You go, and I will order a chamberlain to deliver my decree later."

Zhang Changzong had no choice but to bid farewell to the Empress, and was escorted down the Zetian Tower by four chamberlains.

Wu Zhao watched him leave and then turned to Wan'er.

"When will the infighting in the court come to an end?" She paused for a moment and continued, "Send a chamberlain to deliver the decree, summon Wei Chengch'ing, Cui Shench'ing, and Song Ching for questioning. Also, instruct the chamberlain to inform the three that Changzong has already confessed and his punishment will be reduced accordingly."

Wu Zhao understood that this was a trap deliberately set by people to lure Zhang Changzong in. However, in this situation, she naturally could not continue to protect her lover. She arranged a way for him to escape punishment.

Wei Chengch'ing would not falsely accuse Zhang Changzong of a crime. He casually inquired about the incident, and after completing the investigation, he reported back the next morning during the court session.

"Duke Zhang Changzong of the State of Ye caused trouble with his careless words, and he should be punished according to the law. The sorcerer Li Hongtai ignored the taboos and used evil words to deceive the public, thus he should be executed. "

The Empress nodded in agreement and was about to speak, but the Assistant Minister of Justice, Song Ching, stepped forward and raised an objection:

"Your Majesty, the sorcerer's deceitful words are fabricated to incite discord among people. Zhang Changzong has repeatedly received favor and summoned sorcerers for divination, clearly harboring malicious intentions. He should also be executed according to the law."

The Empress gazed at him with anger. Then, Cui Hsüanhui, the Assistant Prime Minister, and Huan Yanfan, the Deputy Minister of Justice, stepped out and requested the Empress to exterminate Zhang Changzong.

The Empress said solemnly, "Changzong has confessed to me, so he should be pardoned."

The announcement by Wu Zhao, which has long been regarded as law, now received different reactions. The ministers who opposed the Zhang brothers' faction directly challenged the power of the Empress. Song Ching was the first to protest:

"Your Majesty, although the Duke of State of Ye has confessed to his crime, he did not first accuse the sorcerer of talking nonsense. According to the law, he is still guilty."

"Your Majesty!" Feng Quanzhen, the Deputy Minister of Justice, exclaimed loudly, "Zhang Changzong has surrendered forced by the situation, not with his original intention, and the crime of rebellion should not be forgiven. If Zhang Changzong does not submit to severe punishment, why bother with the laws?"

"Your Majesty!" Ma Huaisu, the Inspector of the Imperial Court, also stepped forward and reported, "Changzong betrayed his loyalty and plotted treason, and he should be sentenced to death."

The three of them spoke successively, causing the Empress to become irritated. She understood that they were putting their own interests above those of the state, but in such a critical situation, she could not entirely disregard the advice of these ministers. In her helpless plight, she looked upon the Minister of the Interior, Yang Zaisi.

Yang Zaisi received the hint, announced amnesty of Zhang Changzong, and ordered Song Ching and others to withdraw. However, Song Ching refused to let go of the opportunity to overthrow Zhang Changzong in front of the officials. He thought that victory in this battle was already in sight, so he risked incurring the crime of defying orders and angrily said to Yang Zaisi:

"I only receive the wise decree of the Holy Empress, and there is no need for the Minister of the Interior to announce amnesty."

A stalemate situation emerged in the court, and Wu Zhao immediately realized that it would be difficult to release Zhang Changzong at this moment. Although imperial power is supreme, she must yield to truth in the court discussions.

So the Empress lowered her head and said gently:

"Since Song Ching and others have determined that Changzong is guilty, a reexamination shall be conducted." She paused for a moment, turned to Yang Zaisi, and said in a low voice, "Announce a decree - Zhang Changzong is to appear at the Ministry of Justice for trial."

This announcement was equivalent to admitting the accusations made by Song Ching and others, and condemning Zhang Changzong. The officials all looked at the Empress with different expressions.

So the Empress announced her withdrawl from the court.

After the Assistant Minister of Justice Song Ching escorted the Empress back from court, he personally took Zhang Changzong to the Censorate, thinking he had won completely.

Now, Zhang Changzong was plunged into a desperate terror, fully aware that he had fallen completely into the hands of the dissidents, and his fate would be tragic. He thought of torture, his legs trembling, unable to move forward.

Song Ching looked at him and sneered.

The table of the Imperial Censorate was arranged, and Song Ching solemnly entered the central seat and ordered the trial to begin.

This was a moment that would determine fate. The Central Chamberlain arrives, accompanied by eight chamberlains, standing in the center of the hall of the Imperial Censorate. With an arrogant demeanor, the Central Chamberlain announced:

"Her Majesty the Empress has granted a special pardon to Zhang Changzong - order the chamberlains Feng Wan and Zhang Mingyang to take him away."

So, two chamberlains came out and supported Zhang Changzong, slowly walking out of the Imperial Censorate.

The Empress's power of special pardon was inviolable. Although Song Ching was determined to succeed, he was at a loss when faced with the pardon.

So the Central Chamberlain left behind the decree of amnesty and also exited the hall of the Imperial Censorate.

The victory of the anti-Zhang group was short-lived and immediately disappeared. Song Ching's face turned yellow as he held the amnesty decree, standing there dumbfounded and unable to speak.

After Zhang Changzong left the Southern Court, he finally calmed down, but his robe was already soaked with sweat. He asked the Central Chamberlain to convey his gratitude first, then he would rest for a while before going to thank the Empress for her special grace.

Wu Zhao had returned to the Heavenly Palace. Today's events embarrassed her. She felt that people dealt with Zhang Changzong without mercy, which was essentially going against her. She had to use a pardon to save her lover, indicating a serious violation of the imperial power of the Great Zhou, which she could not tolerate.

Wan'er could see the spasm of anger rising in the Empress, and she was worried!

Soon, the Central Chamberlain returned with a reply, so the Empress felt a bit relieved. She ordered Wan'er to give her a sedative and then lay down on the couch.

As she aged, a wave of anger triggered a severe physical reaction in her. At this moment, she had a severe headache, chest tightness, and could no longer hold on.

When Zhang Changzong entered the Changsheng Hall of the Heavenly Palace, the Empress was trapped in a half-asleep and half-dazed state. Wan'er greeted him outside the curtain and whispered softly:

"For now, let the Empress rest."

"Is her Majesty well?" Zhang Changzong asked sorrowfully.

"Her Majesty is very tired," Wan'er continued regretfully, "Today's incident irritated Her Majesty, and now it seems she has fallen asleep."

"I was wrongly accused."

"Changzong, a tall tree that stands out in the forest will be destroyed by the wind. This is the law of nature. I hope you stop provoking the Empress."

Wan'er earnestly persuades.

He sighed heavily, slumped down, and complained:

"I would like to request the Empress to release me for which I am willing to return my official title."

Wan'er patted his shoulder and said, "Changzong, let's not worry about it. I think we should consider the Empress's feelings."

So they stood facing each other in silence. Before long, Zhang Yichih also arrived. The two brothers were deeply troubled, but when they met, they had nothing to say to each other.

After resting in the inner chamber for a while, the Empress called Wan'er to inquire about the whereabouts of Zhang Changzong.

"He is waiting outside the curtain."

"Let him in!" Wu Zhao closed her eyes again and let out a long sigh.

So Zhang Changzong came in with tears in his eyes and knelt in front of the couch. The Empress touched his cheek, and after a long time, she said gloomily:

"Changzong, as long as I am alive, I will always protect you..."

He sobbed and held the hand of the Empress.

"But I am getting old," Wu Zhao sighed, "I don't know how much longer I can live, while your future is so long ahead!"

"Your Majesty, I will die on the same day as you..."

A melancholic smile appeared on Wu Zhao's cheeks. Today, after the challenge to her authority, her physiological response overwhelmed her ambition. Everyone will grow old and die, but she thought she was exceptional, while her physiological response told her that she was no different from ordinary people, unable to escape the inevitability of aging and death. When the power of will weakened, she felt sorrow, no longer daring to have hope for life.

So, in despair, she murmured softly: "Let me hug you!"

Zhang Changzong leaned into the arms of the Empress.

She was still suffering from a headache and her limbs were still weak, but she forced herself to embrace her young lover.

Psychologically, she saw this as a final indulgence.

Outside the curtain, Zhang Yichih caught a glimpse of this scene, gestured to Wan'er, and walked out.

"How is it?" Wan'er followed and asked softly.

"It's nothing, I'll go back."

"Yichih." Wan'er pondered for a moment before calling out softly.

In an instant, the past reappeared, and Zhang Yichih looked at this beautiful maid in confusion. He first met Wan'er in the Heavenly Divine Palace, when he was frivolously pursuing the joy of youth. Now, he has entered middle age, and life experiences have made him lose the passion of his youth.

The maid-in-waiting in front of him has also lost her youthful vigor. Although she still retained her beauty, she was like a blooming flower approaching the time of withering.

The past of the Heavenly Divine Palace was like just yesterday, however, everything has changed, and Hsüeh Huaiyi, the creator of the Heavenly Divine Palace, has long passed away.

"It's like a dream!" Zhang Yichih murmured.

Wan'er seemed to be emotional, gazing at him for a long time, and then said slowly:

"Happy days like that will never come again."

Zhang Yichih shuddered at these words, realizing that the Empress's vitality could no longer engage in leisure. So he spoke again, heavily: "I'll go back..."

Wan'er held back her tears and nodded.

Zhang Yichih did not leave the Heavenly Palace - the Empress summoned him back and asked him to stay in the Heavenly Palace to accompany her.

This was a spectacle of lingering beauty, the strange psychological response of the aged Empress, who desired to embrace both her lovers while she still could.

The elderly rely on strong spiritual power to support their bodies. Now, the spiritual power of the aged Empress has collapsed. At 10 o'clock at night, Zhang Changzong came out from the inner chamber and woke up Wan'er, asking her to summon the staff of the Imperial Medical Department.

"How is the Empress?" Wan'er asked in surprise and doubt.

"Has fever, body aches all over, and looks very tired." Zhang Changzong said despondently about the Empress's condition.

Chapter 19

The spring rain continued. This was early spring, while it rarely rained at this time in previous years, but this year's climate was abnormal. At the beginning of the year, Luoyang experienced two days of scorching heat as in mid-spring and then it started to rain continuously.

As the Luo River rose, many low-lying areas beyond the city walls of Luoyang were flooded.

The spring rain continued to fall.

- This is the first month of the fifth year of Chang'an era in the Great Zhou Dynasty.

Empress Wu Zhao, who founded the Great Zhou Dynasty, has just recovered from a serious illness and was watching the rain from the corridor of the Shen Gong Pavilion in the Heavenly Palace.

During the winter of the fourth year in Chang'an, the Empress was ill most of the time, and she did not attend court for a whole month. On New Year's Day, she presided over the New Year's celebrations, but due to exhaustion from sitting for so long, she lay down for three days.

The Empress was suffering from old age and illness, and there was no need to hide the fact by now. All the officials in the court and the people of Luoyang knew that the Empress did not have much time left.

Wu Zhao, the Empress of the Great Zhou Dynasty, was already 81 years old. She entered the Palace at the age of fifteen and became a talented lady of Emperor Taizong. Later, she became a consort of Emperor Gaozong and then became the Empress, laying the foundation for her earth-shaking career. As time passed, she rose from an Empress to an Empress Dowager and then from an Empress Dowager to an Empress Regnant, founding a new dynasty. It has been 66 years since she entered the Palace. Nine tenths of her contemporaries have passed away, and she was the only one who remained. However, her life was almost over.

She seemed to have been blessed with good health. Before the age of 79, she was strong, energetic, and people could not see any signs of aging on her. She had always used cosmetics to conceal her age, and at that time, people had the misconception that she was a woman under sixty. However, starting at the age of 79, her body underwent significant changes. This recent serious illness seemed like a big storm that washed away the brilliance of her life. Countless wrinkles appeared on her neck. Age spots covered her cheeks, and her arms were only covered with loose, wrinkled skin wrapped around her bones.

Her hearing and vision have both significantly declined. Now, when speaking to her, one had to raise their voice or she wouldn't be able to hear. However, she tried her best to hide the deterioration of her faculties.

Now, she was watching the rain on the wide corridor of the Shen Gong Pavilion.

She leaned against a silk-cotton cushioned couch, her body and limbs wrapped in a fox fur robe, with only her head and face exposed outside the robe, looking smaller than before. Perhaps it was because the fox fur robe was so ample, or perhaps she has become thinner and shrunk.

Recovering from a serious illness, the Empress was quite slender, with prominent cheekbones and slightly protruding eye ridges. Her deep-set eyes, which were already quite large in proportion to her face, now seemed even more out of place on her gaunt visage. Seen from a distance of nearly 7 meters, one could only see her large eyes flickering.

From her current appearance, no one could imagine that she was a beauty back then.

As the Empress entered and exited in the Shen Gong Pavilion, she was carried by Zhang Yichih, whose senses perceived her body not too far away from that of a skeleton...

However, the Empress was in a good mood in the rain. She enjoyed the rain, perhaps it was an old person's quirk.

To the south of Shen Gong Pavilion, the terrain in the garden was relatively low, and the sewer was blocked, causing the accumulation of several feet of water over an area of about 4000 square meters.

The Empress suddenly became interested in this pool of water and ordered four chamberlains to test its depth. Then, she leisurely said to her two companions beside her:

"I still remember, when I was seven or eight years old, there was a heavy rain, and the yard was flooded. I took a washbasin paddling like a boat and floated in the water. People say that the girls in Jiangnan area pick water caltrops while sitting in a wooden basin." She paused, smiling, "If I hadn't been sick, I would have waded into the water myself to test its depth."

"Your Majesty still has the heart of a child." said Zhang Yichih.

And then, Wu Zhao laughed indulgently. In the past, she had long avoided laughing, but now she no longer cared about it. Even in her laughter, people could see her missing teeth - she had lost two more big teeth due to the serious illness this time.

Four chamberlains were already standing in the water, which was up to their knees.

"Now you can swim," said the Empress, "Can you swim, you two?"

"Changzong can..."

"Your Majesty, Yichih is deceiving you," Zhang Changzong quickly interjected, "He has a conspiracy! He wants Your Majesty to order me to swim now."

The Empress burst into laughter again. Then she reached out a withered hand from her fur coat and grabbed Changzong's hand.

"I won't ask you to swim. The weather is too cold, you'll freeze if you go into the water. I'll let you swim in the summer."

"Your Majesty, I'm really not able to do it," Zhang Changzong chuckled nervously, "I will come to learn this summer."

"It would be great if we were in Chang'an, the water in the Hot Spring Palace was warm," she slowly closed her eyelids, "by the way, we once planned to stay in Chang'an for a while, let's go in autumn."

At that moment, Wan'er arrived at the Shen Gong Pavilion and reported to the Empress:

"The Crown Prince comes to pay his respects..."

"Not necessary, let him go back to the Eastern Palace." Wu Zhao was indulging in watching the rain leisurely and didn't want to be disturbed by others.

Wan'er turned around slowly and left.

The Crown Prince waited in the left wing of the lower floor of the Shen Gong Pavilion. When Wan'er announced the imperial decree to exempt morning greeting, he looked around, suddenly opened his arms and hugged her.

"Your Highness, we can't stay here." Wan'er said, pushing him away in surprise.

"Wan'er, I miss you!" The Crown Prince murmured softly, "It was so difficult for us to meet, and now there is no one around."

"No, we can't." Wan'er said, finally wrapping her arms around the Crown Prince. She continued, short of breath, "The Empress is up there, and the Zhang brothers are there too..."

"They won't come down..."

"Your Highness," her slender fingers gently caressed his neck, her eyelids half closed, speaking slowly as if in a dream, "We must be careful - by the Empress's side, only caution can ensure our safety. As long as you truly want me, we have a long future ahead of us." Her words were gentle and humble, yet her expression was sincere and earnest. As she finished speaking, her half-closed eyes flickered, tears glistening on her eyelashes.

"Wan'er, I think about being with you day and night. As long as there is a chance one day, I will definitely do it. I have already told the Crown Princess a long time ago, and she will treat you like a sister.

Although she is jealous when I get along with other women, it's different with you. Wan'er, you are our lifesaver, without your help, we might not have survived until today..."

Wan'er covered his mouth and said with a pretended look of anger:

"I don't allow you to mention this again. I've said it before, you don't listen to me, you..."

"Wan'er..." The Crown Prince leaned in, kissed her, and then said, "Wan'er, I am grateful and will never forget this for the rest of my life..."

In the moment of being kissed, Wan'er murmured softly and pushed him away.

"Your Highness, please don't tease me. I still need to go up and serve..."

The Crown Prince then gently released her.

Wan'er took out her handkerchief and wiped the Prince's lips, speaking softly and delicately:

"You can go back now. I will find a way to inform you if there is anything!"

The Crown Prince nodded affectionately, straightened his clothes, and slowly walked out.

"Your Highness!" Wan'er followed behind him, softly calling out, and when the Prince turned around, she continued, "Let me take a look at you..."

This was a love message.

At this moment, the Empress on the top of the Shen Gong Pavilion summoned Wan'er.

"Let me go first, you walk slowly behind." Wan'er whispered in his ear, and then quickly walked away.

The Empress summoned Wan'er just to inquire about a few lines from Yu Hsin's "Spring Ode." When she saw Wan'er, she smiled and said:

"The three of us were reciting the last paragraph of Yu Hsin's 'Spring Ode': '*Three days' feast by the river's bend, where the setting sun by the river brings out the spirits. Guests drink under the trees, while people cross the water at the sandy shore...'* There are a few more lines after this that none of us can remember. Can you give it a try?'

Wan'er was famous for her memory. As soon as the Empress finished her question, she eloquently continued:

"The narrow sleeves of her shirt are made of thin silk, and she wears a scarf with beads on it. The sun is about to set on the top of the steep mountain, don't return home until you are drunk after three rounds..."

Wu Zhao smiled brightly, as if eager to continue reciting the last two lines:

"The reflection of water in the pond is brighter than a mirror, and the scent of clothes in the house is not as good as a flower."

"Your Majesty," Zhang Changzong sighed and shook his head, "my memory is failing me."

"None of us can compare to Wan'er," the Empress said, her thin hand gesturing slightly, "Give her a cup of wine, and I will drink one too."

"Your Majesty, it's better not to drink." said Zhang Yichih.

"It's nothing, just have a drink to loosen up. I drink every night."

Wan'er took a sip of wine and turned her gaze to the carriage path in the garden - the Crown Prince's carriage was leaving in the rain at that moment.

She took a glance and immediately avoided it. Her affair with the Crown Prince was her secret which had developed in the past half year. When the Empress was ill, the Crown Prince often came to inquire about her health, so Wan'er got close to him, did everything she could to assist and support him, and also, through a special person - Princess Taiping - let the Crown Prince know that she had been secretly assisting him.

She didn't do it for love. She did it for the future. The Empress was seriously ill, and the future would be a different situation. She has made friends with the Crown Prince, which she believed was a good step. She believed that after the Empress fell, she could rely on her relationship with the Crown Prince to continue her glory, perhaps even more glorious than now, because the Crown Prince and the Crown Princess were both mediocre figures, while she, although she knew that she was not as good as the Empress, was confident that she was superior to everyone else in the Palace.

Wan'er was loyal to the Empress, but she did not intend to sacrifice herself for the latter. Therefore, she had plans for her own future. She had to find a way out for herself - not only Wan'er, but many people in the Palace and the court had planned for their future. At one point, even the Zhang brothers did the same. Li Zhe's return to the position of Crown Prince from being demoted as Prince of Luling was due to Dee Renchieh's efforts, but the Zhang brothers also worked towards this goal! The Zhang brothers wanted to leave themselves a way out. However, soon after Dee Renchieh's death, an incident involving the Crown Prince's son transpired. So the two brothers were naturally hopeless in following the Crown Prince's lead. They hoped that there might still be time for them to oust the Crown Prince before the Empress's reign was over, and to replace him with a successor of their own choosing.

Therefore, they were excited when the Empress recovered.

However, the remaining years of the great Empress's life were always sad. Those she had promoted and cultivated, even her lovers, ignored the present and planned for the future. But Wu Zhao herself did not think about the future.

At an age beyond 80, what can one still hope for in life? Moreover, it was after such a severe illness.

On the top of the Shen Gong Pavilion, she seized the present, savoured it fully, for in her mind, only the present was hers.

In addition, she recalled - her life experience was too rich, with every page of her life history radiating brilliance.

Therefore, she recalled...

When an old person is immersed in memories, it means the journey of life has come to an end.

The spring rain continued, and Wu Zhao, who had drunk a cup of wine, had a blush on her cheeks. It looked like the lingering glow of the setting sun.

As the sun set low, her remaining life was reduced to a faint glow.

Xuanwu Gate was desolate in the spring rain, with guards wearing oilcloth hoods standing numbly on the city wall.

The rain created a white mist rising from the square outside Xuanwu Gate.

Li Duozuo, the Grand General of the Right Imperial Guards, rode out of Xuanwu Gate in a carriage with the canopy lowered. The guards only recognized this officer from the emblem on the front of the carriage, and they saluted as he passed by.

The vehicle did not stop and quickly disappeared into the rain on the square.

Soon, Hsüeh Sihsing, a General of the Left Imperial Guards also left Xuanwu Gate in his carriage.

However, General Li Duozuo and General Hsüeh Sihsing were both present in the General's Mansion of the Forbidden Army at Xuanwu Gate! Although their carriages were decorated with official emblems and officially left the city gate, they actually stayed behind - the heavy rain made it easy for them to conceal their whereabouts.

Among the two carriages that passed through Xuanwu Gate, one carried Zhang Chienchih, the Prime Minister of the Great Zhou Dynasty, and the other carried Cui Hsüanhui, the Assistant Prime Minister.

They both sneaked in under the rain in the carriage of General Chinghui of the Imperial Guards, and now they were sneaking out in the carriage of the Grand General and another general of the Imperial Guards.

It was quiet in the military mansion. The guards at the door hung a sign as usual, indicating that the Grand General had left and visitors were not allowed to enter without permission.

In the sealed room, Li Duozuo and Hsüeh Sihsing faced each other in silence, as if waiting for something. Soon, Hsüeh Sihsing asked in a low voice:

"It seems that they have left the restricted area safely."

Li Duozuo nodded, but did not speak.

"It's been calm these days; I don't think anything will happen." Hsüeh Sihsing's palms were sweaty, indicating that he was nervous about the current situation.

"I think - yes." Li Duozuo sighed softly, glanced at the copper pot dripping, and said, "By timing it, they should have left the restricted area and may have turned into East Street from North Straight Road."

Hsüeh Sihsing also shifted his gaze to the dripping copper pot.

Just then, there was a knocking sound at the inner door. Li Duozuo stood up abruptly and went to open the door himself.

Entering was General Li Zhan of the Imperial Guards, with sweat on his forehead (even though it was a cold early spring day), but a smile on his face.

"Is everything okay?" Li Duozuo asked, his voice slightly trembling.

"I saw them safely exit the restricted area and enter the North Straight Road," Li Zhan heaved a sigh, "I was delayed for a while when Wu Youyi suddenly arrived at the city gates. I tried to avoid his questions, fortunately Chinghui turned up and took Wu Youyi away."

Li Zhan, the son of Li Yifu, an early favorite of Wu Zhao, was originally the Right Acting Cavalier Attendant-in-ordinary. After Zhang Chienchih took office, he recommended a group of new generals of the Imperial Guards, including Li Zhan; in addition, there were Prince Jian'an Wu Youyi as the Guard General of the Left Imperial Guards, while Yang Yuanyan, Chinghui, and Huan Yanfan all served as generals of the Imperial Guards. Yang Yuanyan was transferred from an external position, Chinghui was transferred from the Deputy Minister of Right Bureau, and Huan Yanfan was transferred from the Assistant Minister of Justice. Wu Zhao agreed to these appointments for her own reasons - Li Duozuo was a senior general of the Forbidden Army, always loyal and reliable; Wu Youyi was her nephew, closely related to her interests, naturally reliable; while two generations of Li Zhan were cultivated by her. Yang Yuanyan entered from an external position, so he had no party or private relationships in the Xuanwu Gate; Huan Yanfan and Chinghui were against the two Zhang brothers. These people had different backgrounds, and it was unlikely for conflicts to arise when they were put together. Wu Zhao valued the Xuanwu Gate, understanding the Emperor Taizong's reliance on the support of the Xuanwu Gate Forbidden Army generals to seize the throne by raising troops to enter the Palace.

Therefore, during her reign, she never relaxed her control over the Xuanwu Gate. She was willing to admit people from different backgrounds into the Imperial Guards, so that no one could manipulate these forces. As long as the Army of Imperial Guards was safe, the security of the court was guaranteed.

However, due to the difficulty of personnel management, her meticulous arrangements and precautions had loopholes in the final period of her life.

The generals, who were at odds with each other, but mostly united by their respective futures, plotted against the supreme Empress for their own future.

Now, the three people in the military mansion felt relieved because Zhang Chienchih and Cui Hsüanhui went out safely. Of course, this was only a temporary relief, their real challenges were still ahead...

"We need to have everything prepared," said Li Duozuo in a low voice, "Minister Zhang has already made all the arrangements outside. The timing is crucial; the Empress's health is better today than yesterday. It seems that she will officially start governing tomorrow or the day after."

"Grand General, is it tonight?" Li Zhan asked in a subdued tone.

"I don't know, but we will mobilize at any time and reach our destination within an hour."

"Hmm!" Hsüeh Sihsing's palms were sweating more and more, and he asked hesitantly, "Is there still no news from the Palace?"

"We don't need to wait for the inner Palace news anymore," Li Duozuo said with a faint smile, pointing to Li Zhan, "Zhao Cheng'en is on duty at the right gate. Go and inform him of the situation here, tell him to prepare, and ask him to come here at dusk."

Zhao Cheng'en was also a general of the Imperial Guards, and he has long followed Li Duozuo.

Hsüeh Sihsing asked, "Grand General, What about the handling of Zhu, Chen, and others?"

"No need to act for now," Li Duozuo commanded confidently, "they are in our grasp. When the time comes, we shall tie them up and slay them."

- Zhu◇Zhu Fengchang◇and Chen◇Chen Pingchih◇were the Left and Right Generals of the Xuanwu Gate Guards, who were Zhang Yichih's personal subordinates. Although they were only fifth-ranking officials, their positions were crucial. In addition, there were also a Commander of the Imperial Carriages and three captains who were Zhang Yichih's personal followers. However, these people had too few connections with the Xuanwu Gate. Although they held the important position of guarding the gate, they were only given official information on entry and exit which were not of much use. For example, when Zhang Chienchih went out in the Grand General's carriage, they would not know the details. Therefore, Li Duozuo did not take it to heart at all.

"Grand General, how long will it take for our carriages to come back? If the rain stops..." Hsüeh Sihsing was still nervous.

"Don't worry," Li Duozuo said with a smile, "I reckon Wu Youyi will also leave once he finds out that we are both staying in the same mansion."

"Do we have to hide here all the time? Besides, the rain has stopped, can't we take a ride..."

"It's okay even if the rain stops, who will come to check our carriage? It will be back after dusk," Li Duozuo smiled, "Sihsing, you are too nervous."

It was dusk - the heavy rain had stopped.

In the mansion of the Prime Minister Zhang Chienchih, a few officials including Wang Tongchiao, the Internal Director, Yuan Shuchi, the Deputy Minister of Justice, Chi Zhongfu, the Justice Evaluator, and Cui Taichih, the Official in Charge of Administrative Affairs, gathered together, drinking and chatting while waiting for the time to come.

The twilight in the rain arrived particularly early, their chamber already alight with lanterns.

Zhang Chienchih half closed his eyes, sitting against the wall, as if resting and thinking about something.

Wang Tongchiao was the son-in-law of the Crown Prince. Among this group of people, he was the youngest and the most composed, drinking slowly and steadily, cup after cup.

"Tong Chiao, don't drink too much!" Zhang Chienchih advised gently.

"It's nothing, I only drank three cups, usually I can drink twenty cups," Wang Tongchiao raised his empty cup quietly, "Your Excellency, have a little drink to strengthen your courage."

Zhang Chienchih smiled bitterly, but did not drink.

Time seemed to have frozen.

Before long, Cui Hsüanhui, the Assistant Prime Minister, sent Zhu Chingze, the Assistant Minister of the Ministry of Works, to deliver a message. He reported:

"Minister Cui has set off for the Southern Court, and he has instructed me to inform Your Excellency."

Zhang Chienchih opened his eyes wide and stood up suddenly.

"Chingze, did you come in the carriage of the General of the Imperial Guards?"

"Yes, Your Excellency - Minister Cui instructed so."

"That's it!" Zhang Chienchih bowed to the crowd. "May the spirit of the late Emperor in heaven bless and protect the Tang dynasty, which will be restored tonight."

Everyone in the room stood up and bowed in silence.

"Now, let's get into two carriages separately, squeeze in tightly, and don't make a sound." said Zhang Chienchih, leading the way out of the room.

Two military carriages stopped in the courtyard, driven by two captains of the Imperial Guards.

They all squeezed into the carriages and put down the canvas curtains.

The gate of the courtyard opened, and two carriages slowly drove out, passing through the gate of the East Alley, and then sped towards Xuanwu Gate.

Xuanwu Gate Square was quiet and peaceful.

Outside the forbidden area of the Xuanwu Gate Square, there were three outposts, each stationed with over twenty soldiers of the Imperial Guards.

On the roofs of the outposts, there is a small tower each, guarded by a sentinel. In addition, four cavalrymen are often dispatched from each outpost to patrol the square. In case of any unexpected events, they will ignite fire arrows to notify the garrison at the Xuanwu Gate. The distance between the garrison and the outposts is about one thousand meters. The guards at the garrison will have plenty of time to prepare for any reported incidents.

Now, the two military carriages passed through the outpost smoothly.

The rumbling of the carriages broke the silence of Xuanwu Gate Square.

The sentry on the left waved a lantern to signal the guards at the city watchtower.

And then the outer gate of the double city walls linking the left second gate of Xuanwu Gate was opened, and four imperial guards saluted the two uncovered carriages. Then, the inner gate was also opened.

The two carriages drove straight into the military mansion.

The Grand General Li Duzuo, already informed of the report, had opened the main door of the secret chamber. General Hsüeh Sihsing, with a sword at his waist, stood at the door to greet the incoming visitors.

The Grand General looked serious, exchanged a glance with Zhang Chienchih, then turned to Hsüeh Sihsing and said in a low voice:

"You send for the Left and Right Generals of the Xuanwu Gate Guards..." he said, pausing slightly before turning to another general, "Li Zhan, you go deal with the Commander of the Imperial Carriages - and the three captains as well, follow the planned schedule and act as quickly as possible."

General Li Zhan bowed his head in reply before immediately turning away and leaving. Then, two generals of the Imperail Guards, Huan Yanfan and Yang Yuanyan, were ordered to go to their assigned positions...

"Your Excellency!" Li Duozuo respectfully bowed to Zhang Chienchih, "The preparations here have been completed. Please rest for a while, and we can proceed at any time."

"The Grand General's achievements will be remembered in history," Zhang Chienchih said solemnly, "Once General Li Zhan and General Hsüeh Sihsing return, we can set out."

As the darkness settled, it pressed down upon Xuanwu Gate...

At nearly 9 o'clock at night, the wind began to blow, causing the lanterns on the Xuanwu Gate watchtower to sway, while the armored horses clanged in the wind.

Li Zhan and Ching Hui, two generals of Imperial Guards, along with the Internal Director Wang Tongchiao, led sixteen captains to advance first. Following them were Prime Minister Zhang Chienchih, Grand General Li Duozuo, and others, leading five hundred soldiers of the Imperial Guards, marching eastward through the inner road of the north gate, passing through the double-walled city, and entering the Eastern Palace.

At this time, General Huan Yanfan of the Imperial Guards had already passed through the Western Garden and deployed defenses in the western corner of the Eastern Palace. On another route, General Yang Yuanyan of the Imperial Guards led his troops to guard the White Beast Gate.

The front tower of Xuanwu Gate was guarded by the veteran general Zhao Cheng'en. The military office and inner military district were stationed by General Hsüeh Sihsing.

As soon as the lantern of the Eastern Palace was hung out marking the beginning of 9 o'clock, Li Zhan led his men in and began to monitor the chamberlains and maids in the Eastern Palace.

And then Wang Tongchiao hurriedly entered the Eastern Palace with two chamberlains, woke up the Crown Prince from the bed, and haphazardly dressed him in his robes and hat.

"Tongchiao, what happened?" The Crown Prince asked angrily in a tense tone.

"Your Highness, Minister Zhang and General Li have arrived." Wang Tongchiao replied quietly.

"They..." The Crown Prince realized the seriousness of the situation. He looked up and saw Zhang Chienchih and Li Duozuo entering the bedchamber.

"Your Highness!" Zhang Chienchih bowed deeply to the Crown Prince and said, "May heaven bless the Tang Dynasty, the Northern Gate and the Southern Court have united to support Your Highness's rightful position, restoring the prosperity of the Great Tang. Please go out to pacify the people and enter the Palace to eliminate the traitors."

"Your Excellency..." The Prince's whole body trembled. Although this was what he had been dreaming of, the situation was too sudden. He was completely unprepared mentally and looked around anxiously, not knowing what to do.

"Your Highness, the opportunity is fleeting. The Northern Gate Guards are all loyal to you.Your Highness should proceed to the Palace to vanquish these fiendish villains alongside us." Li Duzuo declared in a resounding voice – the villains he referred to, naturally, were the Zhang brothers.

"Her Majesty...Her Majesty..." The Crown Prince stammered, unable to speak fluently. He was afraid of his mother, and he couldn't believe he could easily overthrow the great mother, so he hesitated and couldn't immediately accept.

"Your Highness, the generals have risked their lives to come here regardless of their families. Your Highness cannot hesitate any longer. The Grand General said that the opportunity is fleeting. If Your Highness hesitates again, I'm afraid everything will be lost." Li Zhan said firmly.

"You guys... ugh, you guys..." The Prince looked like he was about to cry but held back his tears. Finally, he gritted his teeth, uttered a "fine," and then said, "Restrain your subordinates, execute the culprit, and do not frighten the Empress."

The Changsheng Hall in the Heavenly Palace was the residence of the Empress.

The Empress had trouble sleeping after falling ill. She went to bed early in the evening but couldn't fall asleep. Usually, Zhang Yichih and Zhang Changzong took turns reciting poetry to her until she entered a drowsy state, at which point the two brothers would withdraw to the outer chamber, and four maids would attend to the Empress in the incense cage.

After the Empress had entered the inner chamber, Wan'er would leave and go to the left side hall of Changsheng Hall first to review the documents for the Empress.

The Zhang brothers retreated to the outer room, changed clothes, and went to the left side hall.

Wan'er put down her brush and greeted with a smile.

"Is there anything we can help with?" Zhang Yichih asked.

"Nothing much today!" Wan'er stretched lazily, "Has the Empress fallen asleep already?" She glanced at the dripping copper kettle, "Time passes so quickly."

"It's not that fast. It's been an hour since Her Majesty got into bed."

"That's considered fast."

"The Empress's health is getting better day by day!" Zhang Changzong smiled, "Prepare to go to Chang'an, Wan'er."

"You go; I don't want to go." she said with a faint smile.

"Could it be that there is a lover here holding you back and not letting you go?" Zhang Yichih approached and held Wan'er's hand.

She quickly pushed away his hand.

"Be serious! You guys are comfortable in Chang'an, what benefit do I have to go there?" she said, sighing softly, "I will be even more miserable in Chang'an than staying here."

"Wan'er," Zhang Changzong shrugged and said softly, "There is something I need your help with. I want to transfer Huan Yanfan and Chinghui out. They are at Xuanwu Gate, and they always feel like a thorn on my back."

"They've only been appointed for a short time; how can they be transferred so soon?"

"So you need to come up with a solution."

"I'll keep an eye on it," Wan'er nodded with a smile, waved to them, "You can go to sleep now."

"Wait a moment, the Empress may not have fallen asleep yet." Zhang Yichih yawned.

"I'm going to bed too!" Wan'er stretched lazily.

"Would you like a drink?" Zhang Changzong asked.

"No." She said firmly, gathering the files on the table.

So the Zhang brothers had to retreat.

Wan'er couldn't fall asleep right away. She entered the incense cage and looked at the Empress who was already in bed. She would come to see the Empress every night as usual before going to bed.

Although she walked quietly to the bedside, the Empress opened her eyes.

"Your Majesty, are you still awake?" Wan'er asked softly.

"I fell asleep, and somehow woke up again - it seems like my heart is beating fast." Wu Zhao frowned, "People shouldn't grow old, when they do, there will be many changes."

"Maybe you're just tired of watching the rain today."

The Empress seemed to disagree with Wan'er's opinion. She struggled to turn her body sideways and muttered to herself, "I don't know why the muscles on the right cheek are twitching. Will there be any accident?"

"Of course there will be no accidents."

The Empress yawned, "Hmm. Wan'er, you've worked hard, go to sleep." And then she closed her eyes.

Wan'er walked out back to her own room.

It was 10 o'clock at night.

Suddenly, a jumble of noises came in. Wan'er listened carefully as the sounds approached from a distance, which surprised her. It was impossible for anyone to be noisy at night in the Heavenly Palace.

At this moment, the Zhang brothers also returned to their sleeping quarters on the right side of the hall, equally startled by the disturbing noise.

"Yichih, you go and see what's happening!" Zhang Changzong said.

"You go."

Before Zhang Yichih could finish his words, there was a loud crash - the window lattice shattered, the door burst open, the curtains were lifted, and more than ten soldiers of the Imperial Guards rushed in through the broken window and door, heading towards Zhang Yichih and his brother.

"What are you doing?" Zhang Yichih asked in astonishment.

The crowd did not answer, but approached and captured the two brothers. Zhang Changzong saw that they were wearing the uniform of the Imperial Guards, and he knew that a major change had occurred in the court. Seeing his brother struggling, he said heavily:

"Yichih, don't move!"

Zhang Yichih also noticed the attire. He turned his head and called out anxiously:

"Changzong, they are the Imperial Guards..."

The soldiers of the Imperial Guards had already pushed the Zhang brothers out. Outside, General Li Zhan stood with his sword, surrounded by many soldiers. As the Zhang brothers were escorted out of the inner room, two captains held their lanterns up to their faces and solemnly reported:

"Their identities are verified."

Li Zhan waved his hand and shouted, "Execute them!"

"General Li!" Zhang Changzong urgently shouted at the last moment, "If we can survive, my brothers and I will repay you with everything we have."

A hint of a cold smile appeared at Li Zhan's mouth, but he did not answer. The blade of the captains had already come down.

Zhang Yichih let out an earth-shattering scream.

Zhang Changzong also let out an earth-shattering scream.

The soldiers of the Imperial Guards cheered...

Subsequently, Zhang Chienchih, Li Duozuo, and others entered successively, ordering the Supervisor of the Heavenly Palace to announce their arrival to the Empress.

The Empress had already been awakened in the inner chamber, and Wan'er had also entered.

The main entrance to the Empress's chamber was equipped with double doors, making it difficult for outside noises to penetrate. However, the noise outside was too loud, and the night attendant had already reported the incident to the Empress.

Now, the Heavenly Palace supervisor trembled as he entered and knelt down.

The Empress, aided by Wan'er, sat up from the bed and solemnly asked, "Who is causing the rebellion?"

The Supervisor of the Heavenly Palace knelt on the ground, constantly kowtowing.

At this moment, the front door curtain of the inner chamber was completely opened, and Zhang Chienchih, Li Duozuo, and Li Zhan entered, solemnly bowing to the Empress.

"You are causing rebellion?" The Empress asked sternly - she had already seen behind these three people, beyond the heavy curtains, there were shadows of people and sound of clashing weapons, which naturally meant that the situation was dire and irreparable. However, she remained calm in the face of danger, ignoring the overwhelming crowd.

"Your Majesty," Zhang Chienchih bowed and said, "Zhang Yichih and Zhang Changzong rebelled. We, following the Crown Prince's orders, entered to eliminate the traitors. We were afraid of leaking the information, so we did not dare to inform Your Majesty in advance. Now, thanks to the ancestral spirits, the traitors have been killed. We are aware that we have violated the palace regulations and deserve death."

The Empress felt a shiver from the bottom of her heart, gritted her teeth, and tried to regulate her breathing. At this moment, another group of people entered through the front entrance.

They were General Huan Yanfan and Chinghui of the Imperial Guards, Wang Tongchiao, the Internal Director, and the Crown Prince with a dozen or so captains.

The Crown Prince entered the inner chamber and saw his mother lying on the bed with a solemn expression on her face. His heart immediately raced with fear, making him feel weak and powerless despite being in a position of victory. He knelt down and respectfully greeted her.

The Empress suddenly sat up straight. Although she knew the situation was already lost, she never missed any opportunity. At this moment, she seemed to concentrate the remaining energy in her body on her eyes, staring at her son with disdain.

"Great!" she wanted to scold her son, but in a moment of thought, she felt it was not the right time, so she changed her tone, "The Zhang brothers have been executed, what else do you want to do?" She paused for a moment, then issued a sharp command, "It's over, go back to the Eastern Palace."

The Crown Prince trembled and glanced at Zhang Chienchih who stood still, showing no reaction - he was intimidated by the Empress's power.

"Go back to the Eastern Palace!" The Empress seized the opportunity and issued the command again.

The Crown Prince hesitated and was about to get up...

"Your Majesty!" Huan Yanfan suddenly stepped forward from behind and said loudly, "The Crown Prince has already eliminated the traitors, why should he return to the Eastern Palace! Your Majesty, the late Emperor entrusted his beloved son to you more than twenty years ago. Now, the hearts of the people have long returned to the Crown Prince. We, in remembrance of Emperor Taizong's great kindness and grace, have abandoned our families and risked our lives to support the Crown Prince in fighting the rebels. We hope Your Majesty will pass the throne to the Crown Prince, in accordance with the will of heaven and the wishes of the people."

Huan Yanfan spoke passionately, inspiring those inside the chamber, and they all exclaimed together:

"May Your Majesty abdicate in favor of the Crown Prince, in accordance with the will of Heaven above and the wishes of the people below."

Wu Zhao glanced at the crowd, realizing that she could no longer turn the situation around. With her concentration relaxed, she felt despondent and her eyelids slowly drooped.

"Your Majesty, please issue the decree for the succession." Li Zhan said, bowing.

"Are you also a general killing Yichih?" Wu Zhao sighed, "I have treated you and your father well, I didn't expect you to participate as well."

Li Zhan became uneasy and hung his head.

At this moment, Cui Hsüanhui also entered and reported to the Empress on the bed and the kneeling Crown Prince:

"The Imperial Guards have already taken control of the inner court, ensuring tranquility within the six palaces."

"Hsüanhui!" Wu Zhao called out, "I have cultivated you all the time, and now you are also participating in the struggle for the throne!" She then turned to Zhang Chienchih, "You are eighty years old, still full of energy, I hope you will assist the Crown Prince well."

This was equivalent to announcing the Crown Prince's succession. Zhang Chienchih bowed down, and then asked the Crown Prince to go out and appease the crowd.

Wu Zhao saw the Crown Prince kowtow and rise, then turned and left. Following him, a group of people all exited the inner chamber, and the heavy curtains fell down.

"My useless son!" Wu Zhao collapsed in despair.

"Your Majesty!" Wan'er went through a thrilling incident, and now, with her heart still pounding, she urgently asked, "How should we deal with this?"

Wu Zhao closed her eyes, tears seeping out from between her lids. What else can one do in such circumstances? She was in pain, filled with endless regrets. Now what she pondered over was not the sovereignty or the kingdom, but rather the two lovers who had been killed not long ago. She had tried to protect them with all her might, and had also planned for them after her death. She worried that after she passed away, people would not tolerate the Zhang brothers. Unexpectedly, while she was still alive, people had already become unruly.

She thought she had a pair of big wings that could shelter anyone, but reality shattered her imagination.

She also thought of the people she had nurtured and cultivated on her own, who ultimately betrayed her. For decades, she tirelessly built her empire, she changed traditions, she became the first empress in history. However, her empire, which was so difficult to establish, was destroyed overnight.

Now, it was destroyed!

"Your Majesty..." Wan'er couldn't hold back her tears any longer and cried.

"Alas, fool," Wu Zhao said hoarsely, "no need to weep, for tears fall in vain upon those who stand out from the rest. "

"Your Majesty, people have let you down!" Wan'er said, choking back tears.

"It's not that they let me down – but that I was defeated." she said gloomily. "My illness made me slack off, and they took advantage of it." She sighed deeply, as if she had lost all excitement.

"Your Majesty," Wan'er couldn't calm herself and kept asking, "Shall we..."

"Are you asking if we should just give up?" The Empress responded almost calmly, followed by a deep sigh, "Wan'er, success and failure are both common occurrences. While success is certainly joyful, there is no need to be overly saddened by failure." She paused for a moment, then propped herself up and said, "Go fetch to me a cup of wine."

In admiration for the Empress's composure, Wan'er was filled with genuine reverence. She could not fully comprehend how the Empress still remain calm in such a serious situation where she lost everything in an instant - how incredible!

However, when she offered the wine, she found the Empress's body in spasms - apparently, the great Empress was controlling herself with unparalleled willpower.

Wu Zhao took a sip of wine, closed her eyes, rested for a while, and then said:

"Wan'er, you go outside and keep watch..."

Outside, the soldiers of the Imperial Guards tightly surrounded the Changsheng Hall of the Heavenly Palace, prohibiting anyone from entering or leaving. Wan'er saw seven or eight palace maids standing expressionlessly in the corners of the room. She ignored them and turned to the residence of the Zhang brothers.

The glowing lanterns were as bright as daylight, and two headless bodies lay amidst a pool of blood. Inside the room, there were eight imperial guards standing guard.

So she went back and reported what she had seen.

The Empress covered her face with her hands, trembling violently all over.

"Your Majesty!" Wan'er was shocked by the Empress's agitation at this moment. She couldn't understand why these predictable external situations would make the Empress lose control.

"Wan'er, you tell them to remove the two bodies, do they still want me to personally identify them?" Wu Zhao cried bitterly and said with resentment, "These people lack manners too much, ah, two headless bodies..." she said, covering her face with her hands.

Wan'er was moved. Now she understood that the Empress's agitation was not for the sake of the country, but for love. The loss of the country could be forgotten, but the sight of the two headless lovers' bodies made it impossible for her to calm down.

So, Wan'er walked out of the bedchamber again and asked the captains of the Imperial Guards to move the bodies. She could no longer give orders and had to request for a long time, but the only response received was a request for further instructions.

After Wan'er left again, Wu Zhao ordered the maids on duty in the inner chamber to leave. She opened the drawer of the bedside cabinet, took out a dagger, and slowly pulled the sheath down.

She gazed at the sharp edge of the dagger, contemplating using it to end her own life. She thought that dying at this moment would bring the stigma of matricide to her son; an emperor burdened with the label of matricide would find it difficult to secure his throne. Her power was already lost, her lovers were dead, and living had no meaning. In death, she could still enact a final act of revenge.

So she spread the dagger across her chest - men committed suicide by cutting the throat with swords, or using daggers to cut their stomachs. As for women, they rarely used weapons to kill themselves, but Wu Zhao did not want to die like a woman. However, using a dagger to cut her stomach required great strength, and she doubted if her right hand could achieve the goal. Because of this doubt, her hand hesitated.

Her thoughts swirled and surged in an instant. She thought about how the Palace was under the control of others, how they could declare the death of an Empress as needed, how they could forge a dying decree to deceive the world...

Using death as the ultimate revenge is just one's imagination.

So she slowly inserted the dagger into the sheath.

In the inner chamber, she was alone now.

She looked around and slapped the bed heavily!

She regretted her aging, thinking, "If I were ten years younger, I would still have the energy to fight - people wouldn't be able to put me to death, I would have the possibility of rising again, but I am too old now..." She understood that an old person, with limited time left, was not easy to rally people.

She sighed and finally thought... if it were ten years ago, people wouldn't dare to engage in betrayal.

"It's over..." she murmured, staring at the pattern on the wall.

It was her self-declaration, and after it she felt dizzy. She lay down, and all of a sudden, her whole body relaxed, and she didn't even have the strength to move.

When Wan'er entered again, she saw the Empress staring blankly at the ceiling, her eyes devoid of spirit, and her complexion tinged with a bluish hue.

"Your Majesty, they have taken the Crown Prince to the Zichen Hall," Wan'er reported softly.

The Empress seemed not to have heard, her eyes still staring straight ahead.

The turmoil of the night came to an end before dawn. The bells in the Palace rang as usual.

No matter how things change, dawn always remains the same. It was morning, and the Heavenly Palace was bathed in the new sun after the rain.

The rain-soaked roof tiles and mud evaporated steam under the sun. The soldiers of the Imperial Guards patrolled the imperial garden solemnly and energetically.

Princess Taiping rode in a ceremonial carriage, escorted by General Li Zhan and four captains of the Imperial Guards, entered the magnificent gate of the Heavenly Palace. The guards of the Palace stood at attention and saluted.

Princess Taiping whispered a command to stop the sedan from moving forward, then turned to Li Zhan: "General Li, order them to retreat!"

Li Zhan felt embarrassed and did not answer immediately.

"General Li, have them retreat." Princess Taiping said again.

In helplessness, Li Zhan accepted the Princess's order and signaled to the soldiers guarding the Heavenly Palace to retreat outside the Palace.

"General Li, that's of no use." Princess Taiping murmured softly, "Doing so will only hurt the Empress and make many things more difficult to handle."

"Hmm..." Li Zhan hesitantly murmured.

"Now, you wait here while I go in and hopefully achieve our goal." Princess Taiping said with a serene smile.

Ever since the coup, the Empress had lain in bed with her eyes wide open.

Princess Taiping was accompanied by Wan'er as she entered the inner chamber. She rushed to the bed and knelt down, sobbing as she called out, unable to speak through her tears.

"Zhu'er," Wu Zhao reached out and placed her hand on her daughter's head. She cried, but quickly suppressed her emotions and said slowly, "Tell me about the situation outside, there is no need to be sad about it."

"Your Majesty, Your Majesty..." Princess Taiping grabbed her mother's hand and called out passionately, "Mother, Mother..."

"Zhu'er, don't be sad! Success and failure are part of life. I hope your brother can govern this country well." Wu Zhao sighed softly, then paused for a moment and instructed her daughter to stand up, asking, "Tell me about the situation outside."

Wan'er helped Princess Taiping up.

"Mom," she wiped away her tears and said heavily, "I can't imagine..."

"There are many things that are unexpected, such as, it rained yesterday and today is sunny." Wu Zhao patted the brocade belt, asked her daughter to sit down, and said, "I want to know what's happening outside."

"Outside, everything seems calm," Princess Taiping said slowly, "but before dawn today, they sent troops to arrest Zhang Tonghsiu, Zhang Changqchi, and Zhang Changyi, and beheaded them in front of the public at the south of Tianjin Bridge..."

"Oh, they were all doomed! "Wu Zhao sighed, "Are there any other casualties or captives?"

"Other people arrested were Wei Chengching, Cui Shenching, and Fang Rong. The Crown Prince does not allow indiscriminate arrests and killings! So far, there have been no abnormalities in the streets and alleys. Just now, they took me to the Zichen Hall. These are what I heard in the Hall."

"What about Sansi?"

"It is said that the Crown Prince sent someone to invite Sansi to the Zichen Hall for discussion, but Sansi excused himself due to illness."

"Hmm!" Empress Wu Zhao closed her eyelids. She felt both relieved and disappointed by her daughter's report. It was a contradictory feeling - she was comforted by the fact that there were no disturbances and the dynasty transitioned smoothly, avoiding the calamity of war for the common people. However, for herself, she felt disappointed that no loyal warriors came forward, indicating the emptiness of her power.

In an instant, she missed Lai Chünchen, who had been killed by her own hands. She thought: If Lai Chünchen were here, this conspiracy might have been exposed in advance, or even if not, a war would have erupted at the moment of the coup. She just felt too lonely now.

Princess Taiping looked at her mother, who had two deep cheeks, and her eyes were dull and straight. She couldn't guess what her mother was thinking, and therefore, she could only keep her silence. Next to the mother and the daughter, Wan'er stood woodenly.

After a brief moment of reticence, the Empress gave a low, sultry sigh:

"Zhu'er, I'm nearly reaching the end of my life! I don't need to have regrets in my life!" She seemed to be self-deprecating, and paused a little before asking slowly, "Did the Crown Prince ask you to come here to get my abdication decree? "

Princess Taiping nodded - it was embarrassing to speak out, but, in the presence of her wise mother, she felt it was superfluous to conceal it.

"Oh, and they're being too pushy, why would they need my decree, wouldn't it be enough to actually overthrow me? What's more, they will restore the Li Tang Dynasty, but I am the First Empress of the Wu Zhou Dynasty, that's irrelevant!"

"Your Majesty, it is probably because the Crown Prince showing respect to you."

Wu Zhao shook her head and smiled bitterly.

"Your Majesty, it may be..." Princess Taiping continued hesitantly, "Your Majesty has ruled for many years, and the people of the world revere your wisdom. Without the official decree of succession from Your Majesty, it may lead to chaos."

Wu Zhao smiled again, with a hint of melancholy, and said softly:

"That's why I'm still alive this morning!"

"Mom..." Princess Taiping hesitated, "I thought that my brother would not have any improper thoughts. It was Zhang Chienchih and the others who pushed for this matter. As for harming Your Majesty, I don't think they would dare."

"Zhu'er, you are wrong," Wu Zhao sighed, "they are not afraid of anything, just waiting for the right time. The abdication decree..." She pondered, unwilling to say "Once they obtain the abdication decree, they will act", as it would compromise her identity. After a pause, she continued, "Surely I will issue the decree. It's good that you are here, I will entrust it to you."

"Mother..." Princess Taiping said sadly, hanging her head.

"Wan'er," Wu Zhao turned to Wan'er and said dimly, "draft the abdication decree for me." Then she turned to her daughter, "My affairs are over, my story is over."

After Princess Taiping took the abdication decree of the Empress of the Great Zhou Dynasty, the Chief of the Imperial Residence was ordered to come to inquire, and at the same time, requested the Empress who abdicated to move her residence.

"Where do they want me to stay?" Wu Zhao suppressed her anger.

"Shangyang Palace," the Chief of the Imperial Residence said cautiously.

The once fallen Great Tang Dynasty was revived.

However, the founding Empress of the Great Zhou Dynasty was still alive. Over the past fifty years, Wu Zhao ruled the country, shattering the political dominance of the Guanlong and Shandong factions. Officials from the poor families cultivated by her served as military leaders and civil administrators, or held posts in various districts. This influence was not easy to eradicate. Although many impoverished individuals have succeeded by marrying into prominent Shandong families and elevating their status through their in-laws' prestige, there were still many people who missed the grace of the Empress. While they dare not rebel, their hearts yearn for the past. Thus, rumors of the Empress's imminent return spread in Luoyang and Chang'an, and many people took these rumors seriously.

Wu Zhao in the Shangyang Palace actually lost everything, even her freedom of movement. The Shangyang Palace was nominally unguarded, but its comings and goings were subject to intervention.

Since the incident that night, Wu Zhao had been lying in bed almost constantly. Although she had recovered from her illness, she was reluctant to get up – mainly because her legs were weak and she needed to sit down to rest shortly after standing up. In the past, Zhang Yichih would carry her around, but now the thought of it made her feel despondent. Moreover, she had lost her position, and psychologically, she felt she had no place to stand, so why bother getting out of bed?

The attendants in the Shangyang Palace saw the deposed Empress remain calm. However, Wan'er knew that on the long spring nights, the Empress would toss and turn in insomnia, and Wan'er herself would often hear the Empress's deep and sorrowful sighs, sometimes sending shivers down her spine.

It was a sunny day in spring, and the Imperial Garden was filled with lush greenery. In front of the Changsheng Hall in the Shangyang Palace, there were several camellia trees transplanted from Jiangnan, and they were already in bloom.

The Empress suffered from insomnia at nights and thus was mostly in a deep sleep in the mornings.

Wan'er stood alone in the corridor lost in thought - it has been a month and a half since the incident occurred, and generally speaking, the Palace and the Court have been calm. However, she was aware of the rumors circulating in the city.

In the past month and a half, the new Emperor did not visit his mother, but Wan'er met him four times. These were clandestine meetings between lovers, but each meeting had a different pretext - the Emperor sent someone to invite her, ostensibly to discuss some political affairs that were previously handled directly by the Empress, and the meetings often took place at midnight.

In their last two meetings, the Emperor asked her about the truth of the rumors.

The Shenloong (Divine Dragon) Emperor Li Hsien (formerly known as Li Zhe, now changed his name), had a huge distance between himself and his mother. In his heart, his mother was unfathomable. Therefore, he was still worried about his mother sheltered in Shangyang Palace. Wan'er did not disclose the true situation to her lover. She pretended to be mysterious in order to elevate her status in front of the Emperor. In the future, she would have to look up to the Emperor and rely on him, therefore, she had to lay a good foundation for her future now, the Empress's page of history had already finished, while her page was only starting now, and she naturally wasn't willing to follow the Empress and fall into obscurity.

Now, she stood on the veranda watching the buds of a camellia tree, contemplating...

At this moment, a group of chamberlains in brocade robes slowly approached, with the Chief of the Imperial Residence leading the way. She took a few steps forward to greet them, and then she saw the Emperor.

"The Emperor is here to visit the Empress Emeritus." the Chief of the Imperial Residence said as he bowed before Wan'er in front of the steps.

Wan'er glanced at the Emperor, feeling surprised that their mother-son relationship had reached this point. When the Emperor came to pay his respects, he shouldn't be alone! Therefore, she only made a sound of acknowledgment and did not turn around to report, signaling to the Emperor with her eyes.

So Li Hsien walked up and smiled at Wan'er, saying:

"The courtiers and I have decided to confer a regal title upon the Empress Mother."

The Chief of the Imperial Residence called Wu Zhao the Empress Emeritus, but the Emperor referred to her as the Empress Mother. This contradiction in titles reflected the uncertain status of Wu Zhao after losing power.

"You didn't bring any ministers with you?" Wan'er asked softly.

"Wu Sansi followed along, he will come in, and Zhang Chienchih and Huan Yanfan are together with him."

"I will go and report - Your Majesty, may I ask what title will you confer? I would like to know before I report it."

"Empress[3] Zetian the Great Sage." Li Hsien read out each word.

"Oh," Wan'er was greatly surprised by this title, and she asked in a low voice, "Both you and the Empress are entitled emperors?"

"Mother is the Great Sage, greater than me."

Wan'er understood - that title was just a way to deal with rumors. So she smiled faintly and nodded.

"I'll go report it."

Soon, the door to the inner chamber opened.

Wu Zhao sat on the bed, leaning against the headboard.

The Emperor's sudden arrival caught her off guard, and she didn't have time to put on makeup - naturally, she could make the Emperor wait, but when Wan'er reported about the title, the deposed Empress inexplicably became excited. Perhaps the blow of losing power had robbed her of her wits, or perhaps the ravages of old age had weakened her faculties. After Wan'er introduced the Emperor, Wu Zhao propped herself up, ordered a maid to place two cushions behind her, hastily rinsed her mouth and washed her eyes with antelope horn water, and then summoned the Emperor to enter.

One of the Four Virtues that defined womanhood was beauty which Wu Zhao has always valued the most. Indeed, she believed that only by laying a foundation in beauty could one hope to encompass the other virtues. But today, she forgot her womanly beauty.

As the door to the chamber was opened wide, the supervisor of Shangyang Palace outside cried out in a loud voice that the Emperor had arrived for his morning audience.

Therefore, the Emperor of the Great Tang performed the ceremony of paying respects outside the bedchamber, standing with a bowed body, while the Chief of the Imperial Residence announced the title.

"In the third month of the first year of the Shenloong era of the Great Tang, the Emperor visited his mother at the Shangyang Palace and respectfully bestowed upon her the title: Empress Zetian the Great Sage.

After the Chief of the Imperial Residence finished announcing, the Emperor kowtowed again.

Wu Zhao thought that there would be a eulogy when she was given the title, but there were only a few simple sentences. She was slightly surprised and glanced at Wan'er beside the bed, whispering:

"Summon the Emperor..."

So Li Hsien bent down and entered, kneeling in front of the bed, calling out "Your Majesty" hesitantly. At that moment, he looked up and saw his mother's face - for a moment, Li Hsien almost didn't recognize her as his own mother.

The Empress's face seemed to be composed of several scattered bones, appearing stern and abrupt, while the skin covering these bones was withered and dark, not at all like a living person! The mother-son blood relationship was fermenting in Li Hsien's heart at this moment, and he blurted out:

"The son was unaware that Your Majesty was so exhausted. "

Wu Zhao glanced at her son, but the affectionate words did not resonate with her. However, these words reminded her of her negligence in appearance, and she reproached herself for it in her heart.

As for Li Hsien, after speaking out, he was shocked by his own boldness and stood there in a daze.

At the same time, Wu Sansi, Zhang Chienchih, and Huan Yanfan had arrived outside the bedchamber door to pay respects to Empress Zetian the Great Sage.

In her distress, she ordered Wan'er to deliver words of comfort and condolences, and instructed the supervisor of the Shangyang Palace to set up seats outside the bedchamber for reception - she did not want them to enter the bedchamber and see her disheveled appearance, and in doing so, she conveyed her attitude.

This treatment naturally made Zhang Chienchih feel embarrassed, while the Emperor kneeling in front of the bed also felt constrained as a result.

Wu Zhao had experienced many storms, and her slight unease quickly passed. She looked at her son and asked gently, "Is everything normal in the court?"

"Yes," Li Hsien replied mechanically, "everything is conducted according to the old system, with no changes."

"There is no unchangeable policy in the world." She raised her voice so that the three people outside the bedchamber could hear clearly: "Adapt the way of governance to the times. If the old ways are no longer suitable for the present, they can be changed, but it must be done at the right time and under the right circumstances." She paused slightly and asked again, "How is the situation outside the capital? My abdication should not add to your difficulties, right?"

The Emperor had discussed with Zhang Chienchih and others in order to prevent rumors outside the capital, and came to the Shangyang Palace to add a regal title to his dethroned mother. However, he could not directly express these thoughts, and only vaguely replied:

"With the foundation laid by Your Majesty, both internal and external affairs are well settled."

This sentence made Wu Zhao embarrassed and sentimental. She shifted her gaze away from her son and looked at the three men outside, speaking solemnly and deeply:

"I hope my son can thrive in peace, and I hope you will assist with righteousness to maintain the stability of the country!"

"Your Majesty, Empress Zetian the Great Sage, I, your humble servant, will do my utmost." Zhang Chienchih stood up, bowed deeply, and replied in a loud voice.

Wu Zhao was full of hatred towards this old man who had instigated the coup, but at this moment, her demeanor seemed to appreciate him, nodding gently as she asked in a soft voice:

"Minister Zhang, how old are you this year?"

Zhang Chienchih was taken aback. When discussing national affairs, the deposed Empress suddenly interjected with such a question. What was her intention? Due to his confusion, he momentarily seemed to forget his age. Huan Yanfan, who was beside him, quickly reached out and pulled him, so Zhang Chienchih regained his composure and continued to report:

"I'm 83 years old this year."

"Oh, you are two years older than me. It seems like you have a lot of energy."

With this question and answer, the nature of the conversation changed, and the complex meaning of the audience turned peaceful. She then whispered the word "dismiss" to Wan'er before turning to her son.

"Do you have anything else to talk about?"

"Your Majesty..." Li Hsien called out affectionately, his voice filled with emotion.

Outside the door, the three ministers had already left. Wu Zhao watched their receding figures, sighed deeply and sorrowfully, then turned to her son.

"My time is almost up, I won't compete with you for anything, but remember, people will lift you up and then cast you aside. To be an emperor, you must hold power firmly in your own hands. Remember my words." She paused for a moment and continued, "If you have any doubts, you can ask Wan'er. She has learned a lot from me over the years, and her intelligence far surpasses yours."

"Your Majesty..." Li Hsien almost sobbed as he called out.

"You may go, but beware of Zhang Chienchih. His gaze is not sincere, although talented, he is not trustworthy."

She spoke, closed her eyes - sadness and hatred were waging in her chest. Zhang Chienchih was the murderer who tore apart her dynasty. She knew she couldn't destroy Zhang Chienchih herself, but she timely planted a seed of distrust in the heart of her successor. She judged that this would be useful.

So, the Emperor of the Great Tang sincerely kowtowed and left the chamber.

The title of "Empress Zetian the Great Sage ", although granting her an honor, was of no practical use! The world was already in someone else's hands, and after her son left, she pounded the bed with her thin fists.

Wan'er stood still for a moment and said softly:

"Your Majesty, perhaps the situation outside has forced them to come here and address you with the highest title, Your Majesty, can this situation be utilized..."

"It's over!" Wu Zhao seemed to gather the remaining strength of her life to say, her eyes also widened in a terrifying way, "I let him see my old age, he won't fear me anymore. He will believe that I no longer have the energy to rise again, what does the situation outside have to do with me? People won't be foolish enough to work hard for an old lady who is about to die." Her voice trembled, filled with a desolate feeling, "Politicians, everyone is seeking their own interests! What can an old woman who is about to die do to help them? Wan'er, after today, the rumors will stop." She spoke urgently and painfully, so she couldn't catch her breath for a while.

Wan'er stepped forward and rubbed her chest.

"From tomorrow on, there will be rumors in the city that I may pass away soon..." she said sorrowfully, "Give me a mirror..."

So she saw herself in the mirror, a hideous, skeleton-like old woman, extremely ugly. She hated this appearance and regretted using the mirror to look at herself. Suddenly, she threw the mirror away...

Wan'er was taken aback and exclaimed, "Your Majesty..."

"Remember! As a woman, never let others see your old and ugly side."

"Yes, Your Majesty."

"Remember, even when facing death, you must still apply makeup and rouge! As a woman, you must never be without cosmetics even in death."

"Yes, Your Majesty." Wan'er realized she had lost her composure.

"Remember, my sons are fools, not even one-tenth as capable as me," she sighed heavily, "I killed my two intelligent sons, and the remaining two, Ah Dan is smarter than the Emperor. But those in power prefer an emperor who is like a puppet. Alas..."

"Your Majesty, please take a break."

"No need," she continued excitedly, "Wan'er, it seems that the Emperor is interested in you. My eyesight may be failing, but I can still see the way he looks at you..."

Wan'er felt uneasy as her secret was discovered, she timidly called out "Your Majesty" with her head bowed.

"Remember my failure - if possible, use your wisdom to bring down those five people..." she gritted her teeth and continued, "Zhang Chienchih, Huan Yanfan, Chinghui, Yuan Shuchi, and Cui Hsüanhui..."

"Your Majesty, I remember, and if the opportunity arises, I will do as I am instructed now."

"There's also Wang Tongchiao, my grandson-in-law, and..." She gasped for breath, realizing in that moment how many enemies she had. She couldn't continue, thinking that even Wan'er had power, she couldn't handle it all. And more realistically, at this moment, she didn't even have the strength to hate anymore.

Wan'er helped Empress Zetian the Great Sage lie down.

Perhaps because she talked too much and too quickly, she felt her throat was dry and coughed - with a sensation of moisture and a scent of blood.

Wan'er used a rinsing basin to catch the blood that was spat out by Empress Zetian the Great Sage.

She glanced at the rinse basin, showing no emotion, and closed her eyes, saying slowly: "Really, I will not be in this world for long!"

After the dusk of that day, Empress Zetian the Great Sage fell ill with a fever.

- This was the last time she fell ill in her life.

Epilogue

Li Hsien, after reclaiming power from his mother, adopted the reign name of Shenloong in his first two years on the throne, subsequently changing it to Chingloong.

In the autumn of the first year of the Chingloong Era of the Great Tang, a team of Imperial Guards cavalry set out from Chang'an, passed through the Zhongwei Bridge on the Wei River, and headed towards Ch'ien Mausoleum. Shortly after, another small team of Imperial Guards cavalry, escorting a palace carriage pulled by four horses, passed through the Zhongwei Bridge and headed towards Ch'ien Mausoleum, too.

Ch'ien Mausoleum was the tomb of Emperor Gaozong of the Great Tang, Li Chih. In the autumn of the second year of the Shenloong era, the coffin of the great holy Empress was also buried in Ch'ien Mausoleum, reuniting with her husband underground.

Now, the Emperor of the Great Tang has moved the political center from Luoyang to Chang'an. During the reign of the Empress, Luoyang was the political center, and she rarely returned to Chang'an. Now, Li Hsien stayed in Chang'an.

Following the Emperor to the capital, Wan'er bided her time and finally got the opportunity to offer sacrifices to the deceased Empress on her own.

Her status has changed. She was the most favored and powerful concubine of the Tang Emperor. Her position in the Palace was known as Zhao Rong. According to the Tang Dynasty's palace system, Zhao Rong is a rank of second grade, only below the Empress and concubines, and above the nine ranks of consorts. However, since Li Hsien did not have a formal concubine besides the Empress, Zhao

Rong effectively held the highest position in the Palace under the Empress.

Status was not important to Wan'er. What matters was actual power. She controlled the Emperor and manipulated the Empress. Empress Wei became her close friend. She found a lover for Empress Wei with whom they both share. So she has become the actual ruler in the Palace, proclaiming herself as the successor of Empress Zetian the Great Sage.

Therefore, after returning to Chang'an, she had to make a trip alone to the Empress's tomb. There were too many things to report to the Empress's spirit, and she felt that the Empress, who was buried underground, was her only confidante.

She arrived and got off the carriage in front of the Zhuch'üeh (Vermilion Bird) Gate of Ch'ien Mausoleum.

Inside the Vermilion Bird Gate was the tomb passage of the Ch'ien Mausoleum. Passing through the towering trees on both sides of the road, there are a pair of flying dragon horses; twenty steps away, there is a pair of vermilion birds, and further inside, there are ten stone horses standing on both sides of the road; moving further in, there are stone statues, with ten on each side; after walking this section, there is the Memorial Tablet standing on the roadside, leading to the inner gate of the mausoleum. Upon entering the inner gate, the mausoleum passage widens significantly, with statues of foreign tribal leaders on both sides, showcasing the deceased's military achievements. Finally, the Mausoleum Stele appears, with two stone lions standing on its left and right.

She entered the main hall from the right side.

Sixteen chamberlains lined up holding wine offerings. The official in charge of Ch'ien Mausoleum announced loudly and guided her in performing the grand ceremony at the Mausoleum of the late Empress.

She gazed at the tablet of "Empress Zetian the Great Sage", bowed again, and then stepped back. Slowly, she walked around the hall of offerings to the back, staring blankly at the vast and desolate Liangshan Mountain.

The chamberlains stood fifty steps away from her.

She wandered in the cemetery, trying to concentrate her mind and get focused.

The tall trees in the cemetery swayed in the autumn wind.

For a long time, Wan'er's heart seemed to merge with the Empress underground, and she spoke gently and peacefully:

"Your Majesty, Empress Zetian the Great Sage - it's been three years, and I've finally fulfilled your expectations."

The wind was blowing; the wind was blowing...

"Your Majesty, I report to you..." she looked up at the sky and continued slowly, "In the second year of the Shenloong era, on the last day of the third month, Wang Tongchiao, the Emperor's son-in-law, concurrently the commandant-escort, the General of the Right Thousand Guards, and the Duke of Lang County was killed. In the same year, in the ninth month, Zhang Chienchih, the Prince of Hanyang, Huan Yanfan, the Prince of Fuyang, Chinghui, the Prince of Pingyang, Yuan Shuchi, the Prince of Nanyang, and Cui Hsüanhui, the Prince of Boling, were killed. Your Majesty, that year, these five were the instigators of the rebellion. Although they were granted princely titles after their success, I made them suffer until their deaths."

The wind was blowing; the wind was blowing...

"Your Majesty, back then, they seized the Xuanwu Gate and overthrew you. Li Duozuo, who rebelled against Your Majesty with the Forbidden Army back then, revolted again not long ago, but was defeated, lying dead outside the Xuanwu Gate, and his entire family has been exterminated."

The wind was blowing; the wind was blowing...

"Your Majesty, I have long wanted to come, but I have waited until today. I have many things to report." Wan'er said, smiling. She thought that the tasks she had completed in more than three years would be enough to comfort the spirit of the Empress in heaven. She thought that even if Empress Zetian the Great Sage were to come back to life, she might only be able to achieve this much at the same time.

So, she let go of her worries, she smiled at the white clouds of autumn, at the trees in the mausoleum, and at the decaying grass of Liangshan Mountain.

However, the heroic woman sleeping beneath the loess was ignorant of the world, and had no feeling of any gratitude or resentment. Nevertheless, her spirit would live on! The torch has been passed, and Wan'er still remained in this world, smiling for victory...

---

[1] A TYPE OF WESTERN region dances popular in Sui and Tang Dynasty. Zhezhi dance was a vigorous, fast-paced and dynamic dance. It started off as a solo dance, but later evolved into a pas de deux and group dance.

[2] Tao Ch'ien (about 365-427, also known as Tao Yuanming) is a famous Chinese poet from the period of Six Dynasties. His poetry often reflected on the pleasures and difficulties of his reclusive lifestyle.

[3] The Chinese word used here is "Huang Di" which literally means emperor. Wu Zetian was an empress or female emperor, so either the title of Empress or Emperor was proper here.

Did you love *Empress Wu Zetian*? Then you should read *A Story of Consort WateryJade Li 1*[1] by Na Su!

The last memory she had was that she inhaled toxic gas due to the betrayal of her companion in a covert assassination, WateryJade Li heard someone was yelling, partly opened her eyes, noticed everything was unfamiliar, before she could open her eyes fully, she felt something was forced into her brain and heavy about her head, then fell into sleep again. When she opened her eyes again, she noticed people around with shattered clothes of ancient time, why she was in the place of an ancient time, then she realized she had a time travel. A young maidservant called her Princess, as she did not know much information about the princess, then she pretended had a percussion, thus she could forget every related information. Before she could get her body

1. https://books2read.com/u/bOjBWA

2. https://books2read.com/u/bOjBWA

recovered a bit, she heard galloping sounds of horses, people around began to scatter and run for lives, a batch of soldiers were chasing to kill with arrows. She bumped into her future bridegroom Prince Qi when she was straggling the head of the soldiers within a forest, then they together came across the bullying of people by the daughter of a castle owner, then a group of assassins with a blue fox head tattooed on their buttock, then an assassination by people and a pack of wolves in Royal Palace, then an illusory maze set up for her by someone, could Consort WateryJade Li survived the whole process in a time when people were treated as grass and butchered like pig and sheep with another person's body and mission?

www.ingramcontent.com/pod-product-compliance
Lightning Source LLC
Chambersburg PA
CBHW022009150726
47990CB00002B/582